I0456337

AFTERNOON DELIGHT
BOOK ONE

A COLLECTION OF SHORT ROMANCES

TIMA SMITH

amarok books

AFTERNOON DELIGHT
BOOK ONE

amarok books
ISBN: 978-1-944932-15-2

This book is dedicated to Elinor Nauen,
the first editor to say, "yes!"

AFTERNOON DELIGHT
BOOK ONE

STORIES

PERFECT SENSE

I open the door. It's Gary. I had a feeling. Maybe because nine out of every ten times I open the door, he's the one standing there. I stare at him while I count to seven ... long enough to let him know I'm not overjoyed. But I don't know why I bother, because even while we were together he was never good at taking hints. And now that we're separated, nothing's improved. I fold my arms. "What do you want."

"Hay, Mandy." He leans against the door jamb and smiles. "How's things?"

I feel myself going hot around the edges. Nobody can do it the way he can ... make me so mad so fast. "Is that why you rang my bell?" I ask. "Right in the middle of my stress-reduction yoga?"

His eyebrows arch. "Since when do you need stress reduction?"

"Since my life took a decidedly stressful turn," I say. "Maybe you remember? Seven years ago? The day we got married?"

He stands up straight, shoves his hands into his jeans. "Well," he says, "I don't get it. I mean, I thought stress reduction was the reason you moved out in the first place. I figured by now you wouldn't have a stressed cell left in your body." He smiles a little. "Unless things haven't turned out quite the way you'd hoped?"

"My hopes have nothing to do with it," I tell him. "My problem is that I don't seem to have moved far *enough* away. The source of my stress keeps *showing up at my door!*"

We stare at each other.

"Now will you please tell me what you want and then go back to your side of the house?"

"Jeez, Mandy," he says, "you'd think I bugged you all the time."

"You do bug me all the time."

He looks hurt. "This is the first time I've knocked on your door in a week."

"More like three days. Did you not bring me my mail on Wednesday?"

"I thought I was doing you a favor. A neighborly favor."

"What you did was interrupt my dinner. Which was just plain rude. Especially since I had a guest. So from now on, just take any mail that comes there by mistake and give it back to the postman."

"That makes no sense," he says. "Besides, how was I supposed to know you had a guest."

"Right," I say, remembering how he has placed himself directly in Stewart's path to my door ever since our very first date. "I'm sure you had absolutely no idea."

"Stewart's a real nice guy," he says. Then, "Anyway, I wanted to let you know that my cable problem should finally be fixed tomorrow ... so if you ever want to ... you know, watch something ... you and Stewart, even ... I can always get lost for a while."

"We're fine without it," I say.

He nods, starts to walk away, then turns back. "Oh, I almost forgot. Can you give Ellie a message when you talk to her next?"

"Gary, she's *your* sister. Why can't you just tell her yourself?"

"Because ..." He smiles that smile of his, the one that got to me in the first place. "... even though she's my sister, she's *your* best friend and the two of you talk all the time and she's still mad at me about ... everything."

It's true. Ellie has been giving him the cold shoulder ever since I moved out. "Okay," I say, "what do you want me to tell her."

"That I ran into Kate. Her old friend. Tell Ellie that Kate's here scouting apartments because she's moving back." He shakes his head. "She used to practically live at our house. Kate. And it was really good to see her." He gets this look on his face. Similar to the one he usually reserves for his Trans Am. "Anyway, tell her I have Kate's number if she wants to give her a call. Maybe that will get her talking to me again."

"I'll tell her."

"Thanks."

He starts to walk away.

"And Gary?"

He turns back. "From now on, I mean it. No more paper deliveries. No more dropping by because you forgot it's just you now and you bought too many bagels. No more messages for Ellie. And no talking to Stewart as though the two of you are best friends, because you aren't. And if you do any of those things, this whole arrangement is off, and I'll do what I probably should have done in the first place ... get my job transfer, move to New Jersey, and put two thousand miles between us."

I don't wait for a response. I close the door. And then, when I should be planning next week's personnel meeting, I find myself wondering about Kate. Ellie has never mentioned anyone named Kate. Who's Kate?

***

"Why do I let him do this to me?" I ask Ellie. I switch my cell from one ear to the other and listen to her silence. I can almost see the look on her face. Ellie's got this strange idea that half of our break-up, mine and Gary's, is my fault.

3

She sighs. She's tired of hearing it all. And despite her impatience with Gary's seeming inability to grow up, he *is* her brother.

"I know," I say. "I should have moved away. I should have left him in traction and said, 'I told you so! I told you if you jumped out of enough planes and raced enough cars and hang-glided off enough cliffs, *this* would happen,' and then I should have walked away. Far away. But I couldn't just leave him like that, Ellie. Not with three broken ribs, a broken elbow, and a broken leg!"

"That was nine months ago," she says. "The leg is fine, the ribs are fine, and the elbow will never be completely fine, but there's nothing you can do about that. So since you're still here, does it ever occur to you that you really *want* him to bother you?"

"That's ridiculous! The smartest day of my life was the day I moved out."

"You mean all the way from 242A to 242B? The other half of the two-family you own together? The one with adjoining walls, the same roof, and a shared back deck?"

"At the time," I say, "it made perfect sense. He still needed help."

"Not anymore, he doesn't."

"Ellie, all he has to do is leave me alone. The way I leave him alone. Have I ever tried to horn in on one of his dates?"

"Far as I know, he hasn't had one. Besides, did you really think he was suddenly going to become shy and retiring? That he wasn't going to keep trying to get you back? That he was just going to quit loving you because you said so?"

"I don't want to talk about this anymore," I tell her. The phone goes silent. "Oh, just one thing," I say. "He left a message for you. About someone named Kate who's back in town."

"Kate? Kate's back in town? Did he say anything else?"

"Just that he has her number."

"Well, I wouldn't expect anything less of my baby brother."

"He said she was *your* friend."

"Yes, she was. My best friend at school. But the two of them were an item for a while. At least until she went off to New York to become an actress."

"An actress?"

"She had all the leads in the school plays. Everyone thought she was great. Plus she had enough self-confidence to give New York a try."

"Did she make it?"

"No. Not as an actress, but she became a pretty big-time model. TV ads and all the big magazines. I'll definitely have to give her a call to see why she's back."

"Well," I say, "I gotta go. Stewart's coming for dinner."

"He's a really nice guy," she says.

It's what everybody says. That he's a really nice guy. And he is. But more than that, he's the exact opposite of somebody else I know. And that's the thing about him I appreciate most of all. He doesn't give me ulcers. I've even stopped biting my nails. Maybe because he wouldn't be caught dead in a parachute or strapped to a pair of fiberglass wings. Would never even think about going around a track at 150 miles an hour.

***

"You look great, Mandy," Stewart says when I open the door. He hands me a bouquet of carnations, steps inside, and takes a deep breath. "Smells great. Do I smell curried lamb?"

Just then there's a thump above our heads and we both look up.

"It's Gary," Stewart explains. "I just ran into him on the way in. He said he'd be up in the attic running cables and not to let him bother us. That it won't take long."

Now, I think. He has to pick *now* to do it, and I wonder if he can hear us up there ... and if maybe that's the whole idea. I tell Stewart to go into the living room, and I go into the kitchen for some cheese and crackers. "If you can hear me," I hiss, "you better stop this right now. Or I swear..."

"Who are you talking to?" Stewart says from the doorway.

"Just myself," I say, with a big smile. "You get into the habit of doing that when you live alone."

He comes over and looks into my eyes. "I don't think it will be a permanent condition," he says. "You living alone. You're too wonderful. And definitely too kissable." Then he kisses me, very softly, very quickly, and I just know that I'm going to get that tingle from one of his kisses any day now. "Anything in here I can help with?" he asks.

I hand him a bowl of crackers and a bottle of wine. "Take this in and I'll be right there."

It's just something you have to get used to, I guess. A different kind of kiss from the kiss you're used to.

Stewart's sitting on the love seat when I bring in the cheese and the glasses. I sit down beside him. "I love the flowers. You're so thoughtful."

He smiles and puts his arm around me. "Then I'll bring them every time." He looks at me for a moment. "You know, Amanda, I've been thinking about you all the time lately."

There's a thump right over our heads.

"I think about you, too," I say.

"Really?" He looks a little surprised, then pleased.

"To tell you the truth, I didn't think I had a chance with you."

"Why not?"

The ceiling creaks and we both glance up. He shrugs and says, "Because I always figured you and Gary would ... you know ... get back together. I mean, he's kind of an exceptional guy."

"Gary?"

"Yeah. Most guys would give their left leg to be able to do what he does. He's good at everything he does. And he does everything. Plus, he has a beautiful wife."

"*Had*, you mean. And he almost lost his own left leg."

"Does that mean you went ahead with the divorce papers? It's all really behind you?"

"First of all," I tell him, "there's no chance or our getting back together. And as for the divorce papers ... well, that's going to happen any day now. And then I'll be absolutely and totally free to move on with my life."

"Is that a promise?"

"That's a promise."

Our lips are about two centimeters apart.

"You don't know how happy I am to hear that," he says, and he plants his lips right on mine.

That's when Gary comes through the ceiling. He lands across from us, right in the middle of the sofa on the other side of the coffee table, almost sitting up, as though he's been right there chatting with us all along. Pieces of the ceiling are everywhere, and there's a whirl of dust in the air.

Stewart lets go of me. "Are you okay?" he asks Gary. "Are you hurt?"

Gary sits there for a second as if he's considering his answer. "I think I'm okay," he says. He pats the sofa and a puff of plaster rises. "Lucky this was here."

"Lucky my foot!" I say. I stand up. "You big jerk! You've been managing to make my life miserable ever since the first day we met! And this is the straw that breaks the camel's back. And in case you're not listening hard enough, I'll say this once, very loudly. *I'm leaving*!!"

Gary stands up. He and I haven't fought in three months and we have a lot of yelling saved up. He finally stomps out and slams the door, which makes all the plaster dust whirl in the air. It takes a while before I notice that Stewart's gone, too. And right after that, I smell my lamb burning.

***

"Need any help packing?" Ellie asks.

I set my cell on speaker so I can keep wrapping glasses. They're the ones Gary's Aunt Martha gave us as a wedding gift. They have the initials G and A etched and intertwined, and we each took four when I moved out of our apartment. "Now I'll have to find someone else whose name begins with A," he said, while I was packing my things that time. He was trying to make a joke. Even though neither one of us felt much like laughing. It makes me remember that he does that all the time. Even with four broken bones, he was saying things like, 'How could I mange to hit the one tree in that big old empty field?' and 'Really Honey, don't cry. It only hurts when I breathe."

"Most of it's done," I tell her. "But thanks."

"So you're really leaving."

"Day after tomorrow."

"What about Stewart?"

"Stewart was never the right one," I tell her.

"Just a real nice guy," she says, "but no fireworks, huh?"

"Definitely no fireworks."

"It's sad," she says. "I guess I always figured that somehow you and Gary would figure it out. I mean, seven years ... that's a long time. And you were happy through a lot of it, weren't you?"

"I don't know," I say. "Maybe. All I can remember are the hours I paced back and forth waiting for him to come home in one piece. And then the one day he didn't."

But even if I'm not going to admit it to Ellie, I have to admit to myself that a lot of it *was* okay. Even more than okay. Like the time we went hiking up Big Cat Mountain on my birthday. I still don't know how he managed to tote that cake for five hours and still keep the fancy flower decorations perfect. And the way we used to climb up onto the garage roof and lie there looking at the stars while he pointed out the constellations ... Taurus the bull; Andromeda the chained lady; Pegasus the winged horse. Pegasus was always my favorite.

After Ellie and I say goodbye and I promise to call as soon as I arrive in New Jersey, I notice the bill for the newly plastered ceiling on the kitchen counter. I consider leaving it in Gary's mailbox or pushing it under his door, but I haven't seen him in almost three weeks now and it makes me think I should give it to him in person and at least say goodbye. When I knock on his door, a tall, lanky blonde opens it. She has eyes the color of the sky. We stare at each other. Then Gary comes up behind her.

"Hi, Mandy," he says. "Kate, this is Mandy. Mandy, Kate."

I nod, try to smile. After a second, I hold up the envelope. "The bill for the ceiling," I say.

He reaches for it. "Thanks," he says.

We all stand there looking at each other.

"Kate and I ran into each other at Mount James," he says. "She hang-glides, too."

I nod again.

"Gary tells me you're moving east," Kate says. "I just moved back here from New York."

"Kate might take your side of the two-family," Gary says. They smile at each other.

I don't really remember what we all said after that. I just find myself back in my apartment sitting on my love seat, thinking that I should feel relieved. After all, Gary is finally over me. He won't be knocking on my door or falling through my ceiling anymore. I can see the two of them living together in this house that Gary and I shared for seven years. Sleeping in the same bed. Hang-gliding together off into the sunset. Drinking together out of glasses with *my* initial on them.

I try not to think about it, try to put it out of my mind. After all, I'm going off to start a new life, too. A life where I won't have to worry about whether or not my husband's going to live from one day to the next. But I can't get Aunt Martha's glasses off my mind. Even in bed that night. I keep thinking about them, until finally I can't stand it anymore.

I'm pretty sure that the back entrance into Gary's kitchen probably still has a broken lock because Gary never remembers to fix things like that. And sure enough it opens right up when I give the knob a funny little twist to the left.

I tiptoe into the kitchen, open the cupboard, and start taking the glasses off the shelf. Knowing him, he'll probably never even notice they're gone. Except just as I'm taking the last glass down, the kitchen light goes on. I freeze.

"Mandy? What in heck are you doing?"

"I just came to get my glasses."

"In the middle of the night?"

"I didn't want to disturb you again."

"But those are *my* glasses. You already took yours, remember?"

"Well," I say, "I'm taking these, too," and start sliding past him toward the door.

"Hold it," he says, putting his hand on my arm. "Why didn't you just ask me for them, like any normal person would."

"May I have them?"

"No," he says.

We stand there staring at each other.

"Do you really think your next wife's going to want glasses with someone else's initial on them?"

"What next wife is that?"

"Oh c'mon, Gary. I met her this afternoon, remember? I met Kate."

"Ohhh," he says. "Kate. Right. Well, I think Alex might have something to say about that."

"Who's Alex?"

"The guy Kate came back here to marry? The guy she might be moving into your side of the house with?"

"Oh."

"Mandy?"

"What?"

"Did I really make you miserable from the very first day?"

That's when I feel my heart break a little. I shake my head. "No."

Alex bought my wings, you know. And I sold the Trans Am."

I don't know what to say, so I don't say anything.

He shrugs. "My leg is pretty good, considering how many places it was broken. And I think I better try to keep it that way, huh? Besides," he smiles at me, "how long can a guy keep going around in circles?"

He takes two of the glasses from me. "Maybe we could have a little wine and talk about it? Just talk?"

We stand there. Gary in his tee shirt and shorts, his hair all tousled; me, feeling all the walls I built starting to tumble down and already feeling a little bit of the old tingle.

There's an excellent chance we're going to see the sun come up. An excellent chance Gary's going to make breakfast. And it reminds me how much I've missed his blueberry pancakes.

———

WITH LEAVES

Brady looked across the living room at her plants, or at least at what was left of her plants. She held her phone against her ear with her shoulder and reached for her list, drew a circle around 'plants' at the bottom and extended the line like an arrow to second place. Right beneath 'ad for w. dress.' Then the phone slipped and fell onto the couch just as she thought she heard it say something. She picked it up. "Hello?"

"Yes." It was a man's voice. For some reason she'd expected a woman to answer. "Is this Classified?" she asked.

There was a second of silence. "Didn't I just *say* Classified?"

"I dropped my phone," she said, wondering why she was bothering to explain at all. "I didn't hear what you said."

He sighed. It sounded like a 'why do I have to deal with dummies like this' kind of sigh. Which made her mad and almost made her hang up. "We'll start over," he said. "Classified."

"Thank you." She wanted it to sound like she didn't mean it because she didn't. She cleared her throat. It was getting to her, placing the ad. Even though she'd sworn not to let it. Primed herself last night while she lay in bed. And again this morning over her coffee and bran muffin. But it was getting to her anyway.

"Which category will your ad be in?" he asked.

She felt herself stiffen. "Under wedding dresses," she said.

"Under what?"

"Wedding dresses. You know, as in wedding and dresses." A ridiculous giggle left over from sixth grade flew up from some dark space inside her and erupted into her throat. She fought it down.

"Wedding dresses...wedding dresses..."

Why did he have to keep repeating it? Was the man a complete imbecile? Then he said, "we don't have a category for wedding dresses."

"Clothing?"

"No. Sorry."

The line went silent while she waited for him to come up with something.

"Sporting goods?" he said.

It took a minute for it to sink in. A joke. So he *was* an imbecile.

"If you did this on line," he said, "you could look at the categories yourself and choose the appropriate one."

"I don't have service," she said.

"Oh," he said.

She closed her eyes and pressed the palm of one hand against her forehead. It was something her mother used to do whenever her father called at five to say he was bringing company for dinner at six. He did it all the time. She thought about the cabbie last night. "Looks like an okay guy," he'd said, sliding the taxi into the flow of traffic. His eyes in the rearview mirror stared at her, studied her, made her nervous. She wanted them watching the road, not watching her. Besides, she knew Philip was an okay guy. More than okay. And she'd just left him standing on the sidewalk, watching her leave, having helped her carry her things down from his apartment. Because sometimes being okay just wasn't good enough.

"Guess you and him are like me and peppers," the cabbie said into the mirror. "I really like 'em, but they give me wicked indigestion."

She'd done her best to ignore him. She didn't want to talk...about Philip, about peppers, about anything. The cabbie shrugged, got the idea and grew silent.

"Look," she said, switching her phone to the other ear, "just put it under miscellaneous."

"Mis-cell-a-ne-ous," he repeated.

"Under 'M'," she said.

"Thanks," he said, "I wasn't sure. So okay, how will it read?"

"Wedding dress for sale," She read from the card. "White silk with lace overlay. Size eight..."

"Whoa. Wait a minute. This isn't my usual job. You'll have to slow down. Can you start again?"

Her hand went to her forehead. So now she had to repeat it all? When every word was like a bee sting?

"And your usual job is emptying the wastebaskets?" she said. The words hung in the silence between them like so many small sonic booms. Even she couldn't believe they'd come out of her mouth.

'Right," he said. "And I finished the floors, too. I'm a fast worker, but a slow typist."

She almost hung up. "Uh...I forget where we were."

"At the beginning," he said, "Wedding dress for sale, white..." He stopped.

"...silk with lace overlay. Size eight."

"Eight," he repeated, putting a question mark at the end.

"Yes, *eight*," she said.

"No, I meant ... is there more?"

She closed her eyes. Almost said yes. Because maybe the last line wasn't important after all. And she certainly didn't want to say it to this idiot on the other end of the line. Not now that she'd made him an enemy. Another enemy. That made three in a little over eleven hours. The taxi driver was the first. Then the guy in 3B; he was the second. Even though she'd been glad to see him, with all her luggage on the sidewalk, where the cabbie had dumped it. Three B was surprised to see her. "Figured you'd moved out for good," he said. He smiled at her. Before Philip, he'd shown interest. They ran into each other in the front lobby all the time, and on the stairs. They had short pleasant conversations. But last night, when he'd deposited the last of her things in the middle of her living room and she looked at it all—three months of her life sitting in a heap—he hadn't seemed to catch her mood at all. He'd started to shrug off his jacket, suggested he fix them a drink. Even had the nerve to act hurt when she told him that if he expected payment for helping her carry her stuff up, then he could send her a bill.

Enemies. At this rate, if she kept it up, they'd soon include the entire male species.

She cleared her throat. "Yes," she said into the phone, "I'm not finished."

She heard him sigh.

"Never worn," she said, "never altered."

She expected retaliation. It was too good an opening to miss. But he said nothing. He asked her name, address, phone number. Then he thanked her for calling and hung up.

Somehow that made it all worse. There were two men out there who thought she was a witch. And Philip ... Philip just thought she was unenlightened. Actually, he'd called her 'highly unenlightened.' And he'd looked at her as though she was suddenly a complete stranger. "I can't believe you're going to cancel the wedding," he kept saying. "Throw away our whole relationship over nothing ... a meaningless tryst!"

A *meaningless* tryst. She flinched just remembering the words.

"*I'm* supposed to be your tryst!" she yelled at him. "I'm the woman you're living with. We're not even married yet and you're already sleeping around!"

And now, after this stupid telephone call, there was someone out there who saw her as some woebegone little castoff not even worth a final trade of insults.

She drew a jagged line through 'ad for w. dress' and glanced at her watch. Nine-fifteen. Philip's Saturday morning handball would be under way. He wouldn't be up for it though. He'd probably been awake all night. He owed her that much. One sleepless night. And the crazy thing was that he still wanted them to get married. He'd said that while she was packing. He didn't understand. He didn't see anything wrong. *That* was the problem, and it always would be. Other women were everywhere. Too many to be ignored. And it was okay with him if she felt the same way. He didn't expect her to play by a different set of rules because in Philip's world, it turned out, everything was permissible. And how, she kept asking herself, had she missed that until it was almost too late?

She threw her pen at the blue overnight bag sitting on the sofa. The announcements were still zipped into the bulging side pocket. They'd each addressed thirty-five, and now she wished they'd waited to put on the stamps. They'd been stacked on Philip's bureau while she packed, two piles of cream-colored envelopes bound with red rubber bands, emitting all that hopeful energy. Impossible to ignore while she pulled stray socks and underwear from under the bed and Philip argued at her from the doorway. At the last minute, she'd grabbed them and stuffed them into the bag along with everything else.

She'd pictured herself burning them. Standing in front of a fireplace, throwing them in, one by one. Satisfaction, like alcohol on a cut. She glanced around the living room. She didn't have a fireplace, and somehow she didn't think sending them down the garbage chute was going to feel quite the same.

The phone rang and she jumped. Her palms went wet, her mouth dry. But it was only Sara. "He always was a bum," Sara said. "Classy, but a bum. I'm coming over."

***

"I'm displacing," Brady said, snapping the scissors at the papery brown things that used to be the long green leaves on her spider plant. The plants were lined up along the kitchen counter. Even the cactus was wrinkled. The plants in the sink were trimmed back to stubs, soaking water through roots that might be too far gone to care. Worth the try, though. She owed them that much.

Sara fingered a Boston fern and the fronds crumbled onto the floor. "Displacing what?"

"I'm taking it out on every male I see," Brady said. "I insulted a complete stranger on the phone this morning." She turned on the faucet and held the spider plant under the stream. "I have to walk into an office Monday morning where just a little over half the staff are men. And I'm in charge. There's no telling what I might do."

"Oh, c'mon." Sara tried pressing a finger into the cracked soil around the Swedish ivy. "This one's hopeless," she said. "I thought Brian was supposed to be staying here and watering them?"

"My hopeless brother?" Brady said. "And a man, of course."

"Look, today you're drowning in the fact that your life just slammed into a wall. So you've acting like an eleven-year-old. It'll pass. By Monday, you'll be a grown-up again."

Brady set the spider plant on the counter. She turned off the faucet. "When he asked me to move in, I thought it was his way of pledging his fidelity. But I don't think he knows what the word means. He told me the woman just happened to be on the same seminar panel. Someone he used to know. That she just happened to be staying at the same hotel. That if he'd been trying to hide it from me, he could understand. And then do you know what he said? That he asked her to answer his phone, and shouldn't that prove to me that he saw nothing wrong with it? And that I shouldn't either?'" She pointed the scissors at Sara. "And then he had the nerve to say *he* expected more of *me*!"

She took the next plant in line and began to clip stalks. "He made me kill my plants."

"Well, technically your brother killed the plants."

Brady carried two of them over to the balcony. "Help me hang these up," she said.

"Hang them up? You're going to hang these back up?"

"Reminders," Brady said, "of what can happen when you open your heart and turn off your brain."

"They look ridiculous," Sarah said, when they were all back in place.

"They'll come back," Brady said. Although she wasn't sure she believed it.

"If you're willing to live with these, what are you going to do if he calls and says he's seen the error of his ways?"

Brady sighed. "I know the difference between a mostly-dead plant and a completely-dead relationship." Still, she'd missed him this morning when she woke up. And all the plans—the wedding, the honeymoon, the rest of her life. She felt as though she'd just become used to playing a new game, and now it had been replaced by one with rules she no longer understood. It all left her feeling as though she was standing at an angle to her own life.

"There's a terrarium near my desk at the office," Sarah said. "I'll get some cuttings for you."

***

Weeding Dress For Sale. She stared at the ad, felt herself go into a slow burn. *Weeding* dress. She banged her mug down on the table, sloshed coffee right and left. She scanned the rest of the ad. Everything else was right. Except her phone number. She read it again, letting it stew inside for a while. Was this his retaliation? She called work and told Harriet she'd be late.

"Wedding preparations?" Harriet asked.

She'd have to tell everyone not to bother holding the date open anymore. Especially before they organized an office shower. But it would have to wait until she was ready. "I'll see you at ten, Harriet," she said.

***

"We'll be happy to make corrections and run it again." The woman looked across the counter at Brady. "We had a contract problem last week and the person who took your ad was probably just filling in. Not used to the procedure." She fluttered her hand as if any reasonable person would surely understand. But Brady didn't want to understand. She didn't feel like being reasonable. She had all this wonderful anger inside waiting to be vented.

"If I can't see the person who took my ad, then I want to see someone in charge."

The woman looked around. People working in the room buried their heads over their desks. "Just a minute, please."

She left Brady standing there and returned almost immediately with a man in a brown corduroy jacket. He didn't look like someone in charge. He was lanky. His hair was too long. And he smelled like he'd been smoking a pipe.

"You have a problem?" he said. "Maybe I can help."

Brady pointed to the ad. He read it. Brady sniffed. The smell of the pipe tobacco made her think of sitting on her father's lap on Sunday afternoons while he watched the football game on TV. She took a deep breath.

He smiled at her. "Weeding dress?" he said.

"I don't think it's amusing," she said.

His smile faded. "No," he said, "I guess not."

"Furthermore," she said, "I'm quite sure it was intentional."

His eyebrows rose. "Intentional?"

The room went quiet, as if everyone had suddenly stopped breathing. Paranoid. That's what they'd all say after she left. But she didn't care. Maybe, in fact, she'd make a career of it. Confirming everyone's impressions of her. Witch. Paranoid. Highly unenlightened.

He gestured to the pass-through at the end of the counter. "I think we can take care of this better in my office."

She didn't see why. She preferred to stay right there, squared off across the counter like opponents on a court. But before she could say a word, he was disappearing around the corner. He thought she was a wacko and wanted to keep any ruckus she might make as hidden as possible. She followed him, adding wacko to her list.

He was waiting in a doorway at the end of the hall. Adam Craig, she read on the door, Assoc. Editor.

He closed the door behind her. The room hovered somewhere between advanced disarray and chaos. He lifted a folded sweatshirt and a pair of sneakers off a chair. "I run on my lunch hour," he said, putting them on the floor.

She sat down. He sat down. He leaned back in his chair and it gave out a screech. "Needs oil," he said, and smiled.

She began to concentrate on keeping her indignation intact. She could feel its edges going fuzzy, as if the room was chemically dissolving it. He reached across his desk and picked up his pipe, lifted it toward her in a silent *do you mind if I light up?* "It's fine," she said. The smell drifted and she was suddenly eight years old and her father was hugging her because the Rams were winning.

"The person who took my ad is an imbecile," she said.

He narrowed his eyes, puffed. She wanted to grab the pipe and throw it out the window. She wanted to press her nose against his jacket and take a deep breath.

"The person who took your ad," he said, "is me."

She stared at him. His smoke drifted toward the ceiling. "Adding together the time we were on the phone and today, we've spoken to each other for maybe a total of seven minutes," he said. "Would you agree?"

She nodded.

He cradled his pipe in one hand and looked at it, then looked up at her. "And in those seven minutes, you've called me an imbecile twice."

She prepared herself for a duel. But his manner was confusing … calm, unhurried, not angry. Totally deceptive.

"On the phone," he said, "you may only have implied I was an imbecile, but I did get the message." He leaned forward and the chair screeched again. "Do you realize it takes most people twice that long to reach the same conclusion?"

His words registered. And then she did the most unexpected thing. She laughed.

"I may be guilty of mental incapacity," he said, "that I readily admit. But there's not a vengeful bone in my body." He pointed the stem of his pipe at her. "Those errors were stupid. Not intentional. And I absolutely apologize for being an imbecile."

Brady felt the dregs of her anger leak away like air from a balloon. He'd deflated her. And now that the anger was gone, there'd be nothing between her and all that pain. She sighed. "I guess I wasn't in the best of moods that day," she said. "I apologize for being rude."

"Well, I wasn't in best form either," he said, "but that doesn't excuse the fact that our service was less than satisfactory. Please allow us to run the corrected ad free of charge for two consecutive weeks?" He puffed on his pipe. "Is that agreeable?"

She nodded. She got up, wondering how long her clothes would hold the smell of his tobacco.

***

A week later, Brady opened her front door until the safety chain went tight. "*The Swap* has initiated a new policy," he said, through the opening. "Home visits to check on whether or not our services are satisfactory." She slid the chain along its track and opened the door. She smiled. "I guess I have to say 'Not'."

"Now don't be hasty." He stepped into the living room, closed the door behind him, handed her a copy of *The Swap*. "Fresh off the press," he said. "Look under 'W'. As in wedding."

She turned the pages. Her ad was there. Correct. Under its very own heading. "Nice," she said. "Thank you."

He was looking at her half-dead plants. Sara was right; they *were* ridiculous. And she had a crazy impulse to explain. A crazy feeling he'd understand. But before she could get a word out, the doorbell rang again.

Philip looked exactly the way she always thought of him. Polished. Sophisticated. On the move. And seeing him like this, so unexpectedly, took her breath away.

"Hi," he said. "Okay if I come in? I'd have called, but I was on my way to the airport, going right by. Thought you wouldn't mind?"

She found her voice. "Why would I mind? Where are you off to this time?"

"San Francisco," he said. "Two-day symposium."

What she wanted to say was, *why are we doing this? Talking like two old friends on a subway platform just passing the time between trains?*

Then Adam cleared his throat and they both turned to look at him. Brady had forgotten he was there. He smiled at Philip, came over with his hand out, "Adam Craig," he said.

"Philip Granby."

"And I was just leaving," Adam said, moving to the door.

"No," Philip said. "I'm the one who has to run. Got a plane to catch." He turned back to Brady and thrust a small carton at her. "Some things of yours," he said. "Thought you might need them."

She took it. His look reminded her of the Cheshire cat. It didn't bother him at all to find a man in her apartment. In fact, it seemed to please him. She looked in his eyes, searching for something she herself had been feeling...pain, loss, anger, hope...but his eyes were empty of any of those things.

Inwardly, she shuddered. How could she ever trust herself again after having misjudged this man so completely?

"Thanks," she said. "Enjoy the symposium."

"I will," he said.

She closed the door after him. She felt surprisingly normal. Maybe it was good, seeing the ghost in daylight. Maybe it brought the specter down to reasonable proportions and displayed its lack of substance.

Adam stuck his hand in his coat pocket and pulled out his pipe. "Join me on your balcony?"

She nodded. They stood near her plants and looked at the park across the street. The pipe smell took away her tension, and for the first time in two weeks, she felt as though she was where she belonged again.

"Before I leave," he said, "I just want you to know that I'm not normally that callous. The way I was on the phone with you that morning."

She set Philip's box on a wicker chair. "I'd just as soon forget it," she said. "I wasn't my most charming self, either."

"Is he..."

She nodded.

They watched a white poodle on a leash prance through the park.

"This probably isn't the right time," he said, "but would you like to have lunch some time?"

She looked at him, saw nice things in his eyes ... humor, understanding, hopefulness.

"Probably not right away," she said, "but maybe you could check back?"

"I'll call," he said.

***

The very next day, she smelled his pipe tobacco as she climbed the stairs to her apartment, and felt her heart catch just a bit. But there was no one in the hall, just a paper-wrapped shape in front of her door. She bent down and peeled back the white wrapper. Green fronds brushed her hand. Lush, Fragrant. She took the folded note and opened it, smiled. *This is a plant*, the note read, *with leaves*.

———

A LITTLE COMPETITION

I look at everything I own, what there is of it, piled in the back of Andy's pickup. "It's going to fall out," I tell him. "Everything on top is going to slide right onto the highway."

"Kate," he says. He sends me a look and flips a rope from his side of the truck to mine. "Will you stop. Everything on this pickup now will still be there at the other end. I guarantee it." He comes over to my side, grabs the rope and ties it tight. "There," he says, "all tied down." Then he gives me a hug. "Now you take it easy little sister, and call every night, okay?"

I nod. This is not the way we were supposed to say goodbye. It was supposed to be quick and easy. *See you at Thanksgiving. Tell Mom I'll call. Bye.*

"You've got that number?" he asks.

I nod again. The friend of a friend I'm supposed to call when I get to Albuquerque.

In my side-view mirror I see him watching until I make the turn at the end of the road. I turn the radio on low, feel sad and excited at the same time. So here I go. New job. New city. New life. I glance back through the window at all my stuff. Three blocks and it's still there. But for the first half-hour, I can't get myself to go over forty-five. After all, it's all the stuff I have in the world: my bed, my bureau, my rocker, the table I stripped forty-one layers of paint from last summer, and more boxes of stuff than I ever would have thought I could collect in twenty-six years.

And somewhere back there, in one of those boxes, is the comb I was holding when Sam told me he was moving out. When I showed the comb to Andy, he looked at it and whistled. "Didn't know my sister was that strong," he said. But then, neither did Sam. Which is why he ended up moving out that very night instead of the two weeks he was planning on.

I've decided to keep that comb forever. So I'll always remember how strong I am when I have to be.

"Let's take up running," Sam had said about a year before.

"Okay," I said, having no idea what was in store for us.

That first day we ran together, we stood on the edge of the park trail, stretching, because that's what everybody who ran did, and then Sam said, "Now you take it easy and I'll wait for you at the end."

Famous last words.

How could we know that I was a natural runner? And how could we know that he wasn't? And what was I supposed to do? Give up something I could do better than he could just because being bested was hard for him to take? Well, sorry Sam. Because I found out that running made me feel fantastic. And running fast made me feel even better. Plus, I found out I could run very fast for a very long time. And I didn't end up training for ten months just so I could indulge Sam's manliness and let him finish that marathon before me.

So now I hope Sam and Suzanne, whose only exercise seems to be getting up and getting Sam another glass of wine, will both be very happy together.

Besides, I'm finished with it all now. My relationship with Sam is something I plan to have a very hard time even recalling before I even arrive in Albuquerque.

I look at my speedometer. Sixty-five. And all my stuff is still where it's supposed to be. On the truck.

The next morning in the motel parking lot, I walk all around the pickup, making sure the ropes are still tight before I get in. It seems to me they all give a little more than when Andy did the same thing yesterday, but since I drove three hours longer than I'd planned, I only have about five or six to go today. And since Andy's such a whiz with ropes and knots, he must have figured in some degree of stretch.

I get lost twice trying to find the apartment, but when I finally get there, I find two nice big parking spaces right out front. Which is exactly what I need to park, since I can't see a thing through my rear-view window with all my stuff covering it up. And while I'm backing in, it occurs to me that I forgot to call Andy's friend, something I was supposed to do an hour ago, so he'd be here to help me when I arrived. Then a horn blasts at me from behind and I slam on my brakes. That's when all the stuff Andy piled in the truck goes sliding off and I can suddenly see out my rear window just fine.

The driver can't get out of his car because my mattress has ridden up over his roof and slipped down over the top of his door. Not to mention the rocker and a table and a split open box of clothes. I just stand there staring at it all because I can't think of anything else to do.

Then the passenger door opens and Jack Black gets out. Well, not really Jack Black, but someone who looks a lot like him. He looks as though what just happened isn't bothering him in the least. "I'm so sorry," I say. "The ropes must have loosened and when I slammed on my brakes…" But then I don't finish because the driver's door finally bursts open and someone who doesn't look like Jack Black at all jumps out. This person looks very very upset.

He looks at his car. Then he looks at me. Then he looks like he wants to say a lot, mostly things I don't want to hear. But he seems to make an effort, like a pressure cooker deciding to hold in its steam.

"I'm so very sorry," I say again.

He mumbles something that might be 'crazy women drivers' and for a moment I think about reminding him that *he's* the one who pulled in behind me before I was finished parking. But then I decide to ignore him, because he apparently suffers from that common affliction, maleness.

He shakes his head. "Let's get all this junk off the car," he says, sounding as if his teeth are clenched, and they lift the mattress off and stand it against the streetlight.

"Just surface scratches," Jack Black says, "good buffing will take them out." The he lifts the table of the hood and his smile slips. "And maybe a little reshaping."

We all look at the big dent. The driver groans. "I have insurance," I say. But it doesn't seem to make him feel any better.

"The car's brand new," his friend says. "We just picked it up." He puts the table down, shrugs, then he smiles again, as though he's actually enjoying the whole thing. "You moving in?"

I nod.

"Hey, Rick," he says. "You hear that? She's gonna be your neighbor." He doesn't seem to realize this is not something Rick wants to hear right now. "Which apartment?" he asks me.

"Number four."

"Your upstairs neighbor," he tells Rick,

But Rick doesn't seem to be listening. He keeps running his hand over his dented hood.

"Well," his friend says, "while Rick is having his nervous breakdown, we might as well introduce ourselves. I'm Tom. He's Rick." He holds out his hand.

"Kate," I say. "And I think Rick is very unhappy."

Tom shrugs. "He was very unhappy *before* it happened, too. So don't feel bad."

"Well," I say, "guess I'll start moving in." I'm anxious to get going because the last thing in the world I want to do right now is stand here talking about Rick and how unhappy he is.

"We'll help," says Tom. "Won't we, Rick?"

I don't wait around. I don't want Tom to help and I especially don't want Rick to help, not that I think he will. Actually, I don't ever want to see Rick again, and it occurs to me that I might spend the next couple of weeks looking for an apartment on the other side of town. But when I come down again, Tom's carrying my table up the stairs.

"You don't have to do that," I tell him. "I can get help. I know someone in town."

"No. I insist," he says, puffing a little. "Rick wanted to help, too, but he figured he should check in with his insurance company first thing."

When the truck is empty, I offer to buy Tom a pizza. "Sure thing," he says, and on our final trip up, he knocks on the door of apartment two. "You want to come with us and get a pizza?" I hear him say. I want to grab him by the collar and tell him that inviting Rick is not what I had in mind at all. But then I hear Rick say no, that he's had enough trouble for one day.

"Rick can't join us," Tom tells me.

"That's good," I say.

"Oh, he's not so bad. You'll have to give him a second chance."

I decide to change the subject instead. "Do you know where there's a good health club nearby?"

***

Within a week, my new life is sorted out. The apartment's perfect, my new job is better than I expected, and I don't bump into Rick even once. Plus, the health club Tom suggested is better than any club I've ever seen.

"HI," I say, climbing on the one free exercise bike. "This is such a great club, isn't it?" I set bike on the highest level, then I back if off a little. After all, it's been a week since I've done much more than hang a picture or move my rocker from one corner to another or run ten miles every evening.

The person next to me starts to say something, then stops. I look at him, and we stare at each other for second. "I hope the insurance company is taking care of everything to your complete satisfaction," I tell him. Then we both look straight ahead.

""My satisfaction," he says, "would be that it had never happened at all."

I pedal for a while, wondering if being obnoxious is something that comes naturally to him or if he has to work hard at it.

"Perhaps," I say, deciding to give him some of his own medicine, "if you hadn't squeezed in behind me before I'd finished parking, it wouldn't have." I try to concentrate on the bike and wish I'd brought my ear buds so I could completely tune him out.

We pedal along, ignoring each other, except that after a while there's not much to be aware of except for the fact that my bike is going a lot faster than his, which is very satisfactory. But then he ups his speed until he's pedaling just as fast as I am.

I think about Sam and the look on his face when he saw me waiting for him at the finish line of our first marathon, and somehow just thinking about it makes me angry all over again. I yawn and turn up the speed to its highest setting. And of course, like a true male, Rick turns his up, too.

After that, we both keep our eyes on the clock and when the time's finally up, we sit there for a while trying not to breathe too hard. I can't get Sam out of my head now. The way he left me for flabby Suzanne instead of being proud of what I'd accomplished. And the more I think about it, the madder I get. I look at Rick. He might not be Sam, but he's pretty close.

I get off my bike. "Guess I'll go do my five miles now," I say, and head for the track.

"Five miles?" he says, coming up behind me. "I usually do five, too."

I turn around and look him in the eye.

"Unless I have a partner for racquetball after," he says. "Then I only do three miles just to save time." He drapes his towel around his neck, looks at me and smiles for the first time. His hair's curlier than I remember and he looks good in a tee shirt. For a second I almost forget what this is all about. Forget that what he just said is not an invitation, but a challenge.

"Do you have a partner today?" I ask.

He shakes his head no.

"Let's play after we run then," and I head for the track. On my way, I wonder if it's worth risking shin splits for. But then I remember his crack about 'crazy women drivers' and how Sam went off with Suzanne after the marathon, and I decide it is. I look at my watch. "I have plenty of time, by the way," I tell him, when we get to the track. "So go ahead and do your usual five miles. That way we'll be done around the same time?"

He doesn't say anything for a second, then "Great, that's just great."

It's eleven-thirty when the club manager knocks on the racquetball window and points to his watch. It's so late, the cleaning people are already vacuuming the rugs.

"Pretty decent workout," Rick says, as though he'd really have preferred another hour or two.

When I shrug, my shoulder cramps. My fingers have already been cramping off and on for an hour,

I head to the right to the women's showers, and he heads to the left. "See you," he says.

"Right," I say, turning to look back at him as he walks away. There's a big canister vacuum sitting between him and the door to the men's showers and I see him hesitate for a second. I know exactly what he's going to do, because it's just too good an opportunity for him to miss, right? I mean, a chance to show himself—and me--how much spring he still has left in his legs. But unless he's been working out four hours a day for ten years, he probably has a lot less spring than I do. And even I couldn't jump a two and a half foot vacuum right now.

"Don't..." I start to say, but it's too late. I watch the entire embodiment of male ego catch its foot on the top of the vacuum and crash smack into the wall.

***

The next evening I stop by his apartment to see how he is. Tom opens the door wide. "Oh, good, you came," Tom says. "Now I can go home and eat."

I try to tell him I don't intend to stay long, but he seems to think I'm the night nurse or something. "Here's Kate," he tells Rick, pulling me into the living room. "She'll keep you company for a while." And then he disappears.

Rick's sitting on the sofa, his right leg in a cast that ends just above the knee. "Thought I'd check in," I say. "See how you're doing."

He looks at his leg. "Great," he says.

"Hurt much?" I ask.

"Only when my heart beats."

It's obvious that this hasn't improved his disposition a single bit, but still I do feel a little guilty. "That was quite a workout last night," I say. He nods and shrugs, as though four hours of intense biking, running, and racquetball is something he does before breakfast every day. "It's actually more than I've done since I was in training," I tell him.

He looks at me. "Training for what?"

"Long-distance running. I do marathons. I've done a few triathlons, too."

"Oh," he says, "I see." He tries to shift his position on the sofa and grimaces. "So was it fun then?"

"Was what fun?"

"Hustling me."

"Look," I tell him, "that's not what I was doing."

"It's okay," he says, "it's not your fault. You were probably just sent by the gods to drive me crazy."

"Don't flatter yourself," I say. "I doubt the gods even know who you are."

We glare at each other. "Typical woman," he says.

"Typical man, I say."

"Just waltzes into my life and waltzes out as if none of it matters."

"Cares about his own precious ego and doesn't give a damn about mine."

He gets a funny look on his face. "I never said I didn't care about your ego."

"Well I never waltzed in and out of your life, either."

We both go quiet. I sit down.

"It was Mary Ann," he says. "She's the one who did the waltzing."

I sigh. "Sam couldn't take it ... that I could beat him every time."

"Really?" He looks at me. "I thought you were fantastic. Fact is, you're the best racquetball partner I've ever played." He tries to sit up straighter and makes a face.

"Here." I get up and put a pillow behind his back. "I think you would have cleared the vacuum if you'd just had a better extension."

"That was one of the stupidest things I've ever done in my life."

"But your form was excellent. Plus you have a very rhythmic stroke."

"Nothing compared to yours." He looks me up and down. "You're in fantastic shape." Then he smiles. "Maybe we should make sure we have our names straight." He puts out his hand. "Rick," he says, "not Sam."

"Kate," I say, "not Mary Ann."

I could swear I hear a 'pop' in the room. You know, the sort of noise you might expect in the cartoon when ghosts disappear. Then his phone rings. "It's Tom," Rick says. "He wants to know if he should come back for a while, maybe stay over in case I need anything."

I shake my head. "Tell him he doesn't have to. I'll stay for a while. And if you need anything during the night, all you have to do is bang on the floor and I'll just run right up."

He thanks Tom and tells him the situation is under control. Then we look at each other and smile.

———

THE PINK BALLOON

When I think about last year, about those long, cold months between October and March, I like to call it the winter of my discontent. It was the winter I ran right smack into reality. The winter I fell in and out of love with Norman. The winter I spent doing things I didn't want to do.

There I was, working in the library five half-days and three evenings a week. Going crazy. All those books coming off the shelf and going on the shelf. Swiping them out. Swiping them in. Everything in order, catalogued, counted.

Even the librarians looked arranged. The trim on Alice's collar was the color of her skirt. Evelyn's pocketbooks always matched her shoes. And the top of Ms. O'Brian's desk looked like nothing was ever allowed to settle more than a moment. Not even dust.

Dennis wasn't all that bad. He was part-time, like me. And working there didn't seem to be his life mission. It seemed more like a place for him to catch up on his sleep. Sometimes I'd find him sitting in the mending room with his cheek resting on a stack of books he was supposed to have finished taping and gluing forty-five minutes ago, dead to the world. I got in the habit of walking by and nudging him whenever I thought Ms. O'Brian was headed his way. It was the nearest thing to intrigue we had.

I hated that library. But it was a steady paycheck and it fit around my schedule of graphic design classes and even gave me time to study if things were slow.

Up until then, I'd been an artist. My specialty was abstracts, large, dramatic oils that hung in small, nowhere galleries and never sold. I also did abstract portraits that no one could understand.

My only paid commission had been a portrait I did for a friend's mother. She told everyone she was having her portrait painted by Eliza Goodwin, a promising artist. She posed in a long white gown, and she didn't want to see it until it was completely finished. "I want the full effect," she said.

I'll never forget the look on her face when the full effect hit her. I ended up keeping the portrait, and she ended up keeping her money, and it seemed consistent with the way things were going with my art career.

Graphic design, I decided, was legitimate, and people paid you money for it. So what if my creative energy was stunted. At least I'd be able to pay my rent.

So there I was, working in reference one afternoon when Norman walked in.

"I want to build a hot-air balloon," he said. "Can you help me?"

It seemed like such a romantic thing to do, especially with winter settling hard and cold into the ground and into the air and into my heart. I could see him floating high and free, going wherever the air currents took him. I wanted to go, too. Finally, here was someone with imagination.

His pants were too baggy. His shirt was wrinkled. His jacket looked as though it wasn't going to make it through another winter. And he needed a haircut. But none of that bothered me. I liked the fact that he was all messed up. All out of order.

"I saw a movie last night," he said, "and there were these two hot-air balloons—purple, red, blue, green—all different colors. They floated over fields and towns and rivers." He talked with his hands, like he was painting a picture in the air. "I decided right then and there that I was going to build one."

Spontaneous, too, I thought. I spent an hour with him, gathering all the material I could find on hot-air balloons. And it turned out to be no waste of time.

"So, Eliza," he said, "when do you get off work?" He smiled at me.

"Six," I said.

I loved Norman intensely for three months. He was like witch hazel on a sunburn. Like a massage after a hard day. But he was also like sand in a desert storm. And after a while, he began to drift away, a little at a time, further and further, until he just wasn't there anymore at all. He never loved me anywhere near as much as I loved him, and he never built that hot-air balloon, either.

On Tuesdays, my first class began at 8:15, which meant I had to go into the city with all the early-morning commuters. And since I got on at the fourth stop from the beginning of the line, it meant I hardly ever got a seat.

The first Tuesday I saw the clown, it had snowed the night before and there were fewer people waiting for the train. I found a single seat and looked out the window. An outgoing car was just pulling in on the opposite track and the windows flashed by mine, fast at first, then slower and slower. That's when I saw the clown. He was looking out his window, too. He looked right at me, and I was so surprised to see a clown that I just stared right back. He rolled away very slowly until I couldn't see him anymore.

He had a sad face. No smile. The corners of his mouth drooped and the corners of his eyes, too. He looked, in fact, as though he was crying, and for a crazy second, I had the feeling I was looking at myself, at the way I felt.

The clown's car stopped. And when it started up again, he was there standing on the other side of the tracks almost right opposite me. He was holding an instrument case in one hand, and in the other, he had a bunch of balloons on sticks. He looked like a painting standing there, all bright reds and oranges and greens against the white snow. Then he shifted the balloons to the hand carrying the case, all except one, a bright pink balloon. He held it up and out to me with that sad, funny face. As if he knew somehow that I needed it.

My hand moved in my lap. I would have tried to reach right through the window, bumped my knuckles against the glass, it the train hadn't started moving then.

I wanted that balloon.

And the picture of him standing there holding it out to me stayed in my mind all through the ride and all through class, so instead of drawing cubes and string, I drew different dimensions of relation. I drew him in different dimensions of relation to *me* and passed it in at the end of class and didn't even care.

The next day, I bought myself a balloon from a person who wasn't a clown. He was standing inside the subway exit, and I took the one pink balloon he had. It was on a string, not a stick, and I carried it into class and tied it to my chair. Then I took it home, and while I changed for work, it bounced against my bedroom ceiling making soft scraping noises. It was a nice balloon, but somehow it wasn't the same.

On the following Tuesday, I stopped and waited for the 'walk' light, then picked my way across the band of thick gray slush to the subway and fit myself into the flow of commuters on the sidewalk. "Hey, look," someone behind me said, "Looks like the circus is in town."

My stomach did a funny little swoop and I looked toward the tracks. All I could see was his orange hair and his peaked yellow hat.

He turned around just as I was approaching, and he looked at me with his sad face and took a few steps toward me. He was carrying the instrument case in one hand, and with the other, he put his hand in his pocket and pulled out a huge floppy purple flower.

"I ran out of balloons," he said.

I took the flower. "Thank you," I said.

A man in a camel-colored coat walked by and clapped the clown on the shoulder. "Hey," he said, "you found her, huh?"

"Is he talking about me?" I asked the clown. "Have I been lost?"

"Guess you only go in early on Tuesdays?" he said.

I nodded.

"Because I was here on Wednesday, Thursday, Friday, and Monday, and you weren't."

"But why?" I said.

"Because clowns are supposed to cheer people up," he said, "and you need cheering up."

I smiled.

"See," he said, "it works."

I smiled again, and the subway car pulled in, drowning out whatever it was he was saying. Then the car stopped and everyone pressed forward toward the doors.

I held my purple flower close so it wouldn't get crushed and moved along with the crowd, and when I glanced over my shoulder, he was right behind me. We moved to the end of the car and stood holding on to the overhead bar.

He looked down at my satchel. "School?" he said.

"Graphic design."

He nodded. "Like it?"

I made a face. "It's all right. Lots of good steady work when I'm done."

"Steady," he repeated. "You make it sound like the flu."

"Are you a steady clown?" I asked.

"Not really," he said. "I'm a part-time clown." He glanced down at his music case. "But I'm a steady musician. Even though it doesn't provide a steady paycheck. That's why I'm a part-time clown."

"What instrument?"

"Clarinet, sax, oboe. But if there was a fire and I could only save one, I'd save the sax. I use the clarinet for clowning."

I set my feet as the car shifted. "Oh," I said, "I see." Even though I didn't really.

"I work for an instrument company," he said. "I go into the schools, do my act, play the clarinet, get the kids high on learning to do it, too. Then the company rents them the instruments. You figure that maybe out of every ten kids that start learning to play, one is going to stick with it all the way to making actual music. And that's not such a bad thing."

"What other things do you do?" I asked.

"At night, I do gigs," he said. "Whenever I can get them. Parties, clubs." He yawned. "Like last night." Then he smiled, which made me notice that even when he smiled, his face said he was sad.

The train pulled into a station and, somehow, more people got on. He was close to me and I could smell the faint odor of his face paint.

"So graphic design is not a passion?" he said.

"It just misses."

"Then what hits?"

"I paint. At least, I used to paint."

He nodded in a way that made me feel he understood.

"This is my stop coming up," I said.

"Mine, too," he said. He followed me off.

"I go this way," I said, pointing to the right.

"Me, too," he said, walking beside me. "So what's wrong with graphic design?"

"Nothing's wrong with it," I said. "It's just that it's a ..."

"A compromise?"

I looked at him. "Exactly."

"Not such a bad one, though," he said. "I mean, if you were going to school for accounting or programming, when what you really wanted to be was an artist, then that would be a reason to be depressed. But graphic design's right up your alley. And it's probably not such a bad thing for an artist to experience a certain amount of creative discipline." He looked at me. "Like me practicing scales."

"You're awfully logical for a clown," I said.

"That's because I'm only a part-time clown."

We stopped in front of the Design Institute. "I go in here," I said. "Me, too," he said, and we both laughed.

"Thank you for the flower. It was nice of you to go to so much trouble to give it to me."

"Next time," he said, "I'll save a balloon for you." He started walking backward down the sidewalk.

"Hey," I said, "what's your name?"

"Cooper," he said.

I waited for him to add something to it. "Just Cooper?"

He nodded. "Just Cooper."

"I'm Eliza."

"I know," he said. "Eliza Goodwin."

I took a couple of steps after him. "How do you know that?"

"Clowns know everything," he said.

"I thought that was Santa Claus."

"Same thing." He waved, turned away.

I watched him until he turned the corner. And right away, none of it seemed real. Except that I still had my purple flower.

I went up the stairs, pulled open the heavy door, went inside, put my satchel on my desk and sat down. Cooper. Just Cooper. And he'd said he'd save me a balloon next time. But how on earth had he known my name? Then the instructor walked in and I fished a notepad out of my satchel, noticed the textbook sticking out with my name written in big fancy block letters across the top of the cover. I smiled. One mystery solved.

The next time we saw each other, he did bring me a pink balloon, which did make me happy. "Do you juggle?" I asked, as we walked along.

"Only with flaming torches," he said.

We walked up Washington Ave. and I wondered what he looked like without the paint, the orange hair, the sad mouth. I turned my face up to the sun. "I think winter is starting to give up," I said. "I can't wait to see trees with leaves, flowers, birds. And I can't wait to get rid of the ten blankets I have on my bed."

"Sounds like we have the same landlord," he said. And then he yawned.

"Another late night?"

"They're all late," he said, as we waited for the light to change. "Played jazz night at a club up town until one. Then I went for a lesson for two hours. Then I played for two hours. Then I slept for two hours. And now I'm on my way to a school."

"A lesson at one a.m.?"

"It's the only mutual time we could find. The guy's the best sax player east of the Mississippi. It's worth missing sleep for."

We spent two minutes agreeing that we'd like to see each other for longer than a fifteen-minute walk and finally found a time on Thursday between noon and one o'clock when we were both free for an hour. For me, it was after a class and before work at the library. For Cooper, it was between two visits to schools.

We met at a bench near the east entrance to the park, and Cooper was carrying a brown bag. "Here," he said, opening it. "I brought lunch. Beef barley soup … very nutritious. And corn bread. Dessert's a surprise."

We spread the food between us on the bench. It was the happiest I'd felt in so long. Happier even than when I'd been happy with Norman. Sitting there with a clown named Cooper, eating soup and corn bread under a lukewarm March sun.

When we were finished, he brought out two M&M brownies. And when those were gone, he pushed up his sleeve and looked at his watch. "Ten more minutes," he said. "How's this for an idea. On Monday afternoon, let's play hooky from whatever else we're supposed to be doing."

I thought about it. The library would survive without me. Besides, I hadn't missed one day in six months. "Okay," I told him. "Let's meet at the Highlands Station at twelve-thirty. We can go to my place for lunch. I have something I want to show you. Something I've been working on."

"What is it?"

"It's a surprise. But there's a hitch. I get to see you without the face paint and the wig, okay?"

He nodded. "Okay."

***

On Monday, I turned the canvas to catch the light so he could get the full effect. "I started working on it the first day I saw you," I told him. "It's not done yet, but close."

He stared at it. The sad mouth drooped a little more at the corners. "It's very colorful," he said.

"It's you!"

"Me?" He stared at it a while longer. "Why is my ear upside down?"

Somehow, I'd expected something different from him. "It's an interpretive rendering." I said. "Why is everyone so hung up on the recognized order of form!"

"Well, it's not *your* ear that's been disordered," he said.

I sighed. "Never mind. You're not exactly in the minority."

"I'm sorry," he said. "If I had time to study it, I think it would start to make a great deal of sense."

I wasn't so sure.

After lunch, we decided to go to the 7th Street art museum. "You can teach me something about formless space," he said.

"Are you going like that?" I asked.

He looked down at his clown costume, shook his head. "I'm so used to it, I forget I'm a clown. Can I use your bathroom? It won't

43

take long. It comes right off." For some reason, I felt ridiculously nervous. And I sensed that he did, too.

I was at the sink when I heard his footsteps behind me. I turned around. I stared at him.

" I tried to tell you after lunch in the park," he said, "but I know I should have told you that very first day."

"What are you doing here?" I said. "Where's Cooper?"

"I'm Cooper," he said.

"You're Dennis!"

"Well, yeah...I'm Dennis. But I'm Cooper, too. I'm really much more Cooper than I am Dennis. I mean, everyone's called me Cooper practically since I was born. No one calls me Dennis except at the library."

All of a sudden, there were tears in my eyes. "I want my clown back," I said.

"I am your clown."

I closed my eyes. I heard Cooper's voice, but when I opened my eyes, Dennis was standing there.

"I really was going to tell you that first day," he said. "I was going to bring in the pink balloon and give it to you at the library that afternoon. I even brought it in. But you have this way of looking at me there like I'm a piece of reference material. Not that I blame you. Most of the time I'm just a walking zombie there." He shrugged. "But you didn't look at Cooper the clown that way. The clown had more impact on you in five minutes than Dennis did in five months. And all I could think was what if I told you I was the clown and it all just fizzled? I didn't want it to fizzle. I wanted to connect with you when I was mostly awake. When I had your full attention." He looked at me. "Does that make any sense?"

He spoke like Cooper. He stood like Cooper. He moved his hands like Cooper. But my eyes still saw Dennis. "I guess so," I said.

"And ever since I got the clown job," he said, "I've noticed this funny phenomenon. I can do things a lot easier inside the paint. I felt a lot more confident with you as a clown. So I kept wanting to tell you and not wanting to tell you at the same time."

We stood there in the kitchen. I noticed that Dennis moved his eyes just like Cooper. Or did Cooper move his eyes just like Dennis? This was going to take time to get used to.

"We finally have a whole rest of a day together and all we're doing is standing here staring at each other," I said.

He smiled. It was Cooper's smile. But different without the sad mouth around it. While we walked to the museum, I kept glancing sideways at him. Dennis had a nice face. That was something I'd never noticed before.

"C'mon, Eliza," he said, "quit staring at me."

"I can't help it," I told him.

"Why?"

The Cooper/Dennis thing was starting to bother me less and less. I shrugged. "I'm thinking maybe I'll try again," I told him. "And this time I'll try to get your ears right side up."

He smiled. We held hands all the way to the museum.

——

COMPATIBILITY

The fortuneteller slaps her cards on the table in some kind of order that makes no sense to me at all. But it must to her, because she makes little noises over each card —'Ahhha' and "Hmmmm — and clicks her tongue. Next to me, Francie nods and gives me a smile that says, Didn't I tell you this was a good idea?

But I'm not convinced.

The only reason I'm here at all is because Francie has been talking about having her cards read ever since I've known her, and I couldn't think of anything else to do for her birthday. It was only supposed to be Francie's cards being read, not mine. But then the clairvoyant offered to read mine for half-price.

I expected it to be different. Expected a dark, tacky room, someone wearing a bandanna around her head and an off-the-shoulder blouse. Someone with red fingernails and smoky eyes. But DeeDee says she's not a fortuneteller. She calls herself a reader. And she's wearing a short, flowered dress and we're sitting on her enclosed porch.

"Love," says DeeDee, putting a finger on the Ace of Cups. She smiles at me. "And a relocation. Your life will soon take a dramatic turn."

Outside, Francie grabs my arm. "Kate, isn't it too exciting for words?"

I shake my head. "She said you were going on a lengthy trip, Francie — when you just extended your contract at work for another eighteen months."

Francie frowns. "Well, I am planning that trip to Atlantic City. And then she said I was still in the process of getting over a painful relationship — and she was right about that, wasn't she?"

"Atlantic City's hardly a lengthy trip," I say. "It's right next door. And practically *everyone's* in the process of getting over a painful relationship."

Francie rolls her eyes. "You'll see," she says. "Just wait until your life takes its dramatic turn.

"I don't want a dramatic turn," I tell her. "I just want someone who won't make my heart pound so hard that I can't hear what my brain is telling me. I want compatibility. I want someone who's going to think like me, live like me, eat the same foods I do."

"Sounds really exciting," Francie says.

She doesn't seem to understand that I'm thinking about all the agonizing relationships I've had to get over in the last few years—especially Brian, the relationship I'm still trying to get over.

Maybe it takes me a while to catch onto things, but I've finally realized my weakness. And I've made myself a promise. There'll be no more passion in my life. Because passion is the thing that clouds my eyes and makes me ignore all those little, flashing 'stop' signals. From now on, I want nothing more than calm, rational companionship.

The next morning I pull onto the highway, sipping coffee and trying to wake up. Once I get up to speed, I find myself next to a car just like mine. It stays even with me, and I don't think about it again until we hit a traffic jam. We're sitting right next to each other and I hear the same music coming from that car that's playing on my own tape deck. That's when I glance over.

"Love," I suddenly recall DeeDee saying. "An attraction of great intensity." Crazy, I tell myself. But when we both turn off at the same exit and then both drive into the same business park, my stomach does a flip-flop. He pulls into the parking lot opposite mine. And then he waves.

It happens the next morning, and the next. And when I leave work Friday afternoon, I'm not surprised that he's standing by my car.

His name is Alex. We make a date to meet in two hours at Tony's. It was his suggestion and it's my favorite restaurant.

While I'm changing for our dinner, my phone rings. "I'm going to Europe!" squeals Francie. "In two weeks. It's company business, but can you believe it?"

Alex and I pull into the restaurant's parking lot from opposite directions at the same time. The first thing I notice is that we're the same height. The second thing I notice is that we're both used to letting someone else take the lead, because when the hostess asks if we want a window booth, we just look at each other and shrug. She gives us a table near the kitchen door.

"I've been telling Sam about you," Alex says.

"Who's Sam?"

"My roommate. He's the one who talked me into waiting for you this afternoon. Normally I wouldn't have done that." He hesitates, as though he's searching for something he's supposed to say. "You don't play golf by any chance, do you?"

We make a date to play the next day.

"I'm glad we've met," he says, holding up his glass of wine.

"Me, too," I say, and we clink glasses.

And I *am* glad. Because we're probably two of the most compatible people east of the Mississippi, which fits right into my new plan for relationships.

Besides the compatibility, Alex is thoughtful. He sends me a one-month anniversary card.

"Cute," Francie says. "But how come it's taken so long for me to meet him?"

"Because you've been traipsing all over Europe for three weeks."

She looks out the window as a car pulls up outside. Then she lets out a low whistle. "Wow. No wonder you didn't want me to meet him. Why didn't you say he was a hunk?"

I go over to the window. "That's not Alex," I say. "He's getting a ride from his roommate. That's the roommate."

She pokes me with her elbow. "Make it a foursome," she says, "and I'll give you a hundred bucks."

I ignore her and head for the door. Everyone gets introduced. The roommate is Sam, and Francie's right about him. When he takes my hand and smiles into my eyes, the entire apartment lurches. We stand there holding onto each other's hand for a second until it seems absolutely necessary to let go.

Alex is totally oblivious to the fact that Sam and I have just been hit by the same tsunami, but Francie has a silly smirk on her face that tells me she's not. Then Alex comes up with the same double-date idea Francie had.

"Sounds like fun," Sam says, "but I have a date with a horse." He looks at his watch. "And I'm going to be late if I don't head out right now. He flashes a smile, and his eyes connect with mine for about five seconds longer than they should.

"Sam's a veterinarian," Alex says.

"An assistant veterinarian," Sam says.

"Better keep Kate away from him," Francie says. "She's allergic to just about every animal on the planet."

***

After Sam is gone, Alex tells us that Sam's moving at the end of the month. "He's setting up practice on the west coast," he says.

"The west coast," Francie repeats. "My goodness." She comes over and stands next to me. "I guess you might call that a 'relocation,' huh Kate?"

I try to pretend I didn't hear her.

"Actually, a rather dramatic turn in a person's life," she says.

That night she calls about thirty seconds after Alex leaves. I picture her sitting upstairs in her living room with her thumb poised above auto dial waiting for the front door to bang.

"So?" she says.

"So what?" I say.

"C'mon, Kate." She sighs. "I was there both times, remember? When DeeDee told you love was going to mow you down? And then again today when you got mowed down?"

"I did not get mowed down," I tell her. "Sam was here for all of five minutes."

"Sometimes that's all it takes."

"Not for me. I've given all that up, remember? Besides, there was another guy there named Alex and he and I are perfectly compatible."

"Sure," she says.

Well, she can say whatever she wants, but I've been the hot-and-heavy route and all it got me was heartache. I intend to ignore the fact that I can still feel the heat from Sam's handshake. Still remember the tingly feeling I got from his look. I intend to resist those things completely.

***

I pull up in front of Alex's place the next day and honk the horn. Sam comes out and squats next to my door so we're face to face. "Hi," he says.

"Hi."

"Alex can't make it for an hour or so," he tells me. He tried to call you but you didn't pick up."

I look at my empty phone caddy. "I knew I forgot something," I tell him.

"He's working on a computer that needs to be on-line by midnight."

"Oh," I say.

"He suggested I entertain you."

We stare at each other.

"We were going to play golf," I say.

"Not exactly my sport," he says.

I should have guessed. Because every man I've ever been attracted to has had absolutely nothing in common with me.

"Tennis?" he says.

I shake my head.

"I'll give you a lesson, then." He stands up, opens my door, and I get out even though I know I should drive off and never give him another thought until he's 3000 miles away.

***

"Tennis is fun," I tell Francie, while we eat popcorn and watch our favorite band on late night TV.

"Everything's fun with the right person," she says.

"That's not what I meant. He's actually the exact wrong person. And it was fun anyway."

She just looks at me. Then I get a text from Alex. "He has to go to Chicago for a week," I tell her. "And we had tickets to a concert on Friday." Then another text comes in. "He wants me to go with Sam."

"The guy definitely has a death wish," she says.

After the concert, Alex texts that he has to go from Chicago to New York and from New York to San Francisco. He's gone three weeks. Sam and I hang out. We play tennis a few more times, go for a hike and have a picnic. He tells me no one is allergic to horses and takes me along to check on a horse that's recovering from an infected leg. And he's right, I don't sneeze once. Then suddenly he's moving to the west coast the next day and I find myself helping him pack.

"This is crazy," he says, zipping up the last bag.

"Too many carry-ons?" I say.

"Not my luggage," he says, "us. We've both been acting like nothing's going on between us. Like all we want to be is good friends." Then he grabs me and kisses me and it's not the kind of kiss one good friend gives to another by a long shot. "Come with me, Kate," he says.

The words *what time do we leave* leap into my mouth, but I don't say them because it's only passion making me feel this way. I shake my head. "It wouldn't work."

He keeps his hands on my shoulders. "Seems to me it would work fantastically well."

"I'm allergic to your profession," I tell him.

"I'll burn my clothes before I come home every day," he says.

"We don't like any of the same things."

"But we like each other a great deal, and what's more important than that?"

"Compatibility," I say. "Shared interests. Stability."

"That's crazy," he says. "You make it sound like some kind of business arrangement."

"It's safer that way."

He looks at me. "Is that what you see in Alex? Someone safe? Someone who'll never hurt you because he can't? Because you don't really care enough to *be* hurt?" He narrows his eyes. "Is that what you think *he* wants, Kate? Is that what you think Alex deserves?"

My eyes get hot and wet. And there it is. The proof that Sam can hurt me, make me angry, make me sad, make me feel things I thought I didn't want to feel ever again. I grab my purse. "You can think whatever you want," I say, heading for the door. "But since you're so concerned about Alex, maybe you should think about what you tried to do to him just now, asking me to go running off with you."

"At least it would have been honest," he says, as I close the door behind me.

That night, Alex comes straight to my place from the airport. "I hope Sam took good care of you while I was away," he says. And it hits me what a sweet guy he is. The kind of guy you want to have as a friend.

"Alex," I say, "I've been doing some thinking while you were gone."

"It doesn't really work, does it," he says. "You and me."

I look at him, surprised. "Maybe not as well as it should."

"The thing is, I met someone in San Francisco. We only saw each other once, but there were sparks. And it made me realize what you and I feel for each other is nice, but not exactly ..."

"Sparky," I finish for him.

"Yeah," he says.

"What if that's all there is?" I ask him. "Just sparks that start to fizzle and go out."

He smiles at me. "But what if they don't? What if the sparks become a fire?"

At five a.m., I'm wide awake. Sam's leaving in half an hour. It takes fifteen minutes to drive to his place, which gives me fifteen minutes to pack whatever I need to move to the west coast for the rest of my life. I pack one bag and write a note to Francie asking her to send the rest. I enclose $20 and tell her to send DeeDee some flowers. "Sorry this is so abrupt," I write, "but you know how it is when your life takes a dramatic turn."

——

CLOSE QUARTERS

Deb pushed through my office door, her arms full of folders. "Guess what?" she says.

I can see it's not something that's going to thrill me. "I'm not sure I want to know," I tell her.

She deposits the folders on my desk. "They just found these behind a file cabinet," she says, and stands there looking at me with her hands on her hips.

"What?" I look at the folders. "But that means all the figures in the report will have to be changed!"

"I know." She plops down in a chair. "I'll stay late to help."

This is a job I moved three thousand miles for, left my fiancée behind for. And if it wasn't for the fact that this company is going to owe me the world after this horrible project is over, I might just get up and head home this very minute.

"Why did they just let him continue handling things this way?" I ask Deb. "The man was ninety-eight years old! He carried a pocket watch, for heaven's sakes." The man was Wellington Sturgis III. His grandfather started the company, his father was president for forty-nine years, and Wellington topped even that.

I sigh and look out the window at the marina. "Oh well, what difference does it make." Looking at the water, the sailboats, the gulls always has that effect on me. How bad can anything possibly be when the Pacific is only yards away.

And office on the harbor. That's what Jeff kept bringing up every time we had a discussion about whether I should put those three thousand miles between us for a year or not. "Look at it this way," he'd say. "It makes perfect sense. We weren't going to make any serious relationship moves for a year anyway. And this is a great career move for you. Important for our future."

"But what about our present?" I'd ask.

"I'll fly out whenever I can. You'll come back for the major holidays." And then he'd hit my major weak spot. "You'll be right on the ocean, Emily. You're always saying how much you miss it."

On my calendar there's a big red circle around December 23. But lately, every time I look at it, I think I should feel more excited than I do. I haven't seen Jeff in almost three months—Thanksgiving wasn't on our list of major holidays. And lately, it's as if I can barely remember the exact color of his eyes. Oh, we were in constant touch for the first eight weeks—texts, calls, Skype. But then he sometimes didn't pick up when I called, started taking hours or days instead of minutes to reply to my texts. And now I'm not all that sure who he is anymore. And frankly, I'm not all that sure who I am, either.

Out in the harbor, a beautiful green sailboat is approaching the dock. I point it out to Deb.

"Wow," she says, getting up and walking to the window, but I know it's the guy at the helm she's talking about, not the boat. "I'm going to take a quick coffee break, and then we'll start on this stuff, okay?"

"Sure." I smile as she slips out the door.

Pretty soon I see her out the window heading straight for the sloop. It takes about four minutes of conversation before he helps her up on deck.

"Nice boat?" I ask, when she gets back.

"Beautiful," she says. "His names' Scott. He's a photographer." She pauses. "He asked if I knew anyone who could sail."

"Why?"

"He need someone to handle the boat while he's shooting photographs. I said you knew how."

"You volunteered *me*?"

"Well you're always telling me what a great sailor you used to be," she says. "Please. Just talk to him? I said we had to work late but we'd stop by when we're done."

I look out the window. It *is* a beautiful boat. It takes her another thirty-three seconds to talk me into it.

It's after eight when we head out, and the air outside is fresh and salty. "Hey, Scott!" Deb calls to the boat.

Scott's head emerges from the companionway hatch. "Hey," he calls back, "I'd almost given up on you."

"This is Emily," Deb says. Scott and I shake hands across the tiny sliver of water between the boat and the dock. "Nice to meet you, Emily," he says. "Won't you both come aboard?"

We get a tour, and it's one of the most beautiful older yachts I've ever seen. All the teak and mahogany shine; the wood and brass steering wheel feels wonderful under my hands. The deck is neat, all the sails stowed, the lines coiled.

"If it's not too late," maybe we could go somewhere for dinner?" Scott says. "You pick the restaurant. My treat." Then he looks at me. "We could talk a little about you crewing for me?"

"We haven't eaten anything since lunch," I tell him, "so I'd like that very much."

But Deb is sitting all hunched up in the cockpit and she makes a funny little noise. "Are you okay?" I ask her.

She shakes her head. "I think I'm going to be sick."

We help her back onto the dock,. Scott gets her a drink of water. We all sit there for a while until a little color comes back to her face.

"Maybe you just need to get something in your stomach," he says.

"No," she says, "what I need is to go home and lay down."

"I'll go with you," I say, standing up and pulling her up, too.

"No," she says. "You stay. I'll be fine. As long as I never get on another boat in my whole life."

We watch her walk away. "That's awful," Scott says. "Have you ever been seasick?"

"Never," I say.

"Me neither." He looks at me. "So. Should we do dinner?" Somehow it doesn't feel right without Deb, and he seems to pick up on that. "Or," he says, "I could just fill you in on what I need and let you get home."

"Let's do that," I tell him. I sit down in the cockpit, look up at the stars, and listen to the water lapping against the hull, while he ducks below to grab "a couple of sodas and a bag of popcorn."

We end up staying there until well after midnight. He tells me about the trips he's made, the photo jobs, the adventures he's had, the storm he had to ride out for three days that had him wondering if he might not make it through.

I tell him I have nowhere near the experience he has, but that I started sailing when I was eight and I can certainly keep this boat on course while he takes his photographs.

"Hired," he says. "As long as you don't mind being here Saturday morning at dawn."

"As long as we don't do this again Friday night," I tell him.

I find it hard to concentrate at work the next day, have to finally close the shade so I can't look out the window. Deb comes in late. She said the bed rocked half the night. "Did you two go out to dinner?" she asks, looking a little wistful.

"No," I tell her. "We just talked for a while and then I went home."

She smiles.

***

Saturday morning, we're out of the harbor before the sun comes up. Scott sets the auto pilot and we eat bowls of granola and yogurt, pour cupfuls of hot milky coffee from a thermos. "Great, huh," he says, when we're out in deep water.

I nod. "Do you ever get lonely when you're out at sea for a long time?"

"Sometimes," he says. "But these are pretty close quarters and so far I haven't found anyone I could really share them with." Then he stands up as the sun floods the sky with a thin layer of rose-colored light. "Time to go to work."

And we work hard for the rest of the day, with only one break for chicken sandwiches, pickles, and cold tea. By the time we sail back into the harbor, the sun is leaving a rosy layer on the opposite side of the sky, and we do a repeat of now slightly soggy sandwiches. But this time the tea is hot, and I know that if I close my eyes for more than a blink, I won't wake up for several hours.

"Can you come back tomorrow?" he asks. "Not so early, if you can't give me another full day. But I'd really appreciate a few hours. "You name the time we start."

I think about my ride home, the few hours of sleep I'll get, the ride back in the early morning dark. "We could start early again if I slept aboard," I say, and then I can't believe I said it. "I mean, if I slept ..." I don't know how to fix it.

"Look," he says, "this is strictly business. I'll sleep up here. I do it all the time. You can sleep below."

He gives me a sleeping bag and a pillow. I'm aware of the motion of the boat for about ten seconds and then I'm fast asleep until I smell coffee eight hours later.

He's bought muffins, and we repeat the granola and yogurt. His hair is totally mussed, his clothes wrinkled, and I realize that's what I am, too. But it doesn't matter because there's no room for vanity on a boat. He washes the bowls, then gives me a thermos of hot coffee. "It'll be cool on helm for a while," he says. I take the thermos and our hands brush. "You're a good sailor," he says. "And good company, too."

"I'm not sure what to say. All I can think about is how blue his eyes are.

By the end of that second day, I feel like I've been doing this forever. I know what course to set before he tells me. He knows when I need a break before I ask for one. We forget about work for a while and watch a pod of pilot whales. He tells me about a job he had once where he sat in a cubicle eight hours a day, how he just got up one Monday and walked out.

"What are you doing over the Christmas holidays," he asks. "I was thinking you might like to spend them here on the boat. No work. Just a sail to somewhere out there." He points to the horizon where the sky and water meet.

It hits me that this invitation isn't something he came to quickly or easily. That inviting someone to share these close quarters is something special. So I tell him about Jeff and realize that I feel as though I'm telling him about a stranger.

"I get it," he says. "And here I was the one telling you it was all business."

We spend the rest of the day mostly without speaking. It doesn't feel strained, but it does feel sad. And when we finally get back to harbor, it's dark and there are a million stars in the sky.

We clean up, stow everything, and he says, "I'm glad we had the chance to meet, Em." It's what he started calling me yesterday. No one except my father ever calls me that. He gives me a hug.

"Me, too," I say.

As I drive home, I notice how solid everything feels. The road beneath the tires, the steering wheel in my hands, and I'm sorry that the memory of these two days is only something to keep, like a souvenir from a beautiful place you visited once and know you'll never be able to see again.

Very early on December 23rd, I'm driving to the airport when I realize I'm going somewhere I *should* go, to be with someone I *should* want to be with, but don't anymore. What if you can plan so hard for the future, I wonder, that you give up all your todays?

What if there's more to life than decisions that make perfect sense? What if there are decisions that just make you happy?

I pull over to the side of the road and call Jeff, tell his voice mail that I'm sorry, but I won't be coming. "I guess we need to talk," I say, "or maybe it's too late for that."

At the dock, I step aboard the boat, knock on the companionway door. "I hear you're looking for crew for a trip over the holidays?" I say.

The door swings open. His hair is rumpled. He's not wearing a shirt. His eyes are as blue as an October sky.

"I only sail with a very special crew," he says. "And she has to be very certain that it's what she wants."

I touch his face. "Oh, she's very certain."

He takes me in his arms, and, all of a sudden, the close quarters feel exactly right.

———

ANOTHER CHANCE

When I hear the bus coming up the road, I go to the window and watch it stop in front of the house. Jason leaps off the top step, waves to his friends, and races for our front door.

"Hey, Mom," he says, tossing his backpack onto the floor. Then he heads straight for the refrigerator.

"Have fun at camp?" I ask him.

He shrugs. "It was okay."

I remember when I used to have to sit down with him for at least half an hour to listen to every little thing that happened during his day. I miss that.

He grabs an orange and a handful of cookies and pours himself a glass of milk. Then he looks up at the clock and slugs the milk down in three gulps. "Gotta go, Mom," he says, heading for the door.

"But you only just ..."

"Gotta help Chris," he calls back to me. "He has to drill about a zillion holes for the electric wires today, and he needs me to help. Bye."

"But what about our ..." He doesn't hear the rest. Strawberry picking. That was the plan. My plan, at least. Although practically since Jason could walk, it's been one of his favorite things to do. I stand there watching his red shirt disappear across the yard. We used to eat more strawberries than we ever brought home, our fingers red from the juice. Still, there were always enough strawberries for at least one pie and several jars of jam. But this summer, it looks as though I'll be picking strawberries all by myself.

I'd give anything to have never met Chris O'Neil at that party last fall, to have never mentioned that the land next to mine was for sale.

I jab the numbers on my cell. "What's up?" Linda says.

"I suppose you wouldn't want to go berry picking by any chance?"

"Not really," she says. "But I could come and watch *you* pick. Give me five minutes, okay?" That's the thing about best friends; they always know what you're really saying, what you really need.

"So," she says, as I start picking strawberries, "it sounds like Jason's gone and done what I've been telling *you* to do for a long time now. He's gotten himself a little male companionship."

"It's not a *little* companionship," I tell her. "He's over there all the time."

"Well, do you blame him?" she says, eyeing me quizzically.

I stop picking and stand up straight to stretch my back. "And what is that supposed to mean?"

"It means he's a nice guy, Katie. I know him. Plus, he's a pilot—a very exciting thing to a ten year old. Not to mention that he's building his own house with his own two hands."

"You forgot something," I tell her. "He plays the guitar. And according to Jason, it's a really awesome guitar."

"Wow," she says. "How much more could a person ask for?"

We look at each other and she laughs. After a second, I have to laugh, too.

Before I fill my pails, she tells me everything I don't want to hear. How I can't expect to be the only person in Jason's life forever. How I should be glad he's found such a wonderful role model. And how not all men are like Jason's father. "You know," she says, "you might have walked away from him eight years ago, but as long as you let what he did to you ruin the rest of your life, then you never really left him at all." She stands up and gives me a very big hug. "Don't let him keep on hurting you, Katie. Give yourself another chance."

After she's gone, I pick a few more strawberries and think about the first time I met Chris O'Neil and how differently things started off between us.

It was a party I didn't even want to go to, but couldn't think of a good excuse not to. It wasn't as bad as I'd thought it would be, wasn't bad at all, actually. It was informal, the people were nice. And then someone introduced me to Chris.

"Do you live in the neighborhood?" he asked.

I shook my head. "I live outside of town, on the other side of the state forest. How about you?"

"I'm just here visiting a relative," he told me, "but I'm thinking of settling in the area." Then he grinned. "Well, not in town—too many houses, too many people." Then he looked at me very intently, so intently I felt my cheeks go hot. "Tell me what it's like out where you are."

"Roads with no traffic," I said. "Lots of mud in the spring. Deer in the backyard."

"Right in your backyard?"

I nodded. "Devouring all our strawberries."

"You have strawberries?"

I nodded again. "Enough for my son and me and half-a-dozen deer."

He looked at me. "Not enough for your husband?"

I felt my cheeks get hotter.

"It's just me and my son."

He nodded. "And the deer."

"And the deer," I repeated.

We smiled at each other.

"It sounds great," he said. "You don't know of anything for sale over there, do you?"

"Not any houses," I said, "but there's a piece of land for sale right next to mine."

He gave me another intense look. "Really."

"Really."

I have to admit that for several days after the party, I just couldn't stop thinking about him. But then I straightened myself out. Jason and I needed another man in our lives the way a dog needed fleas. I told myself to remember that.

Even so, when he called and asked if he could drop by one evening a month or so later, the sound of his voice made my stomach flutter. And when I answered the door and he said, "It's good to see you again," in spite of myself I felt the same way.

He had brought a blueprint of the house he intended to build once the land was his. His hands were tanned and strong, and I got so distracted watching them that I missed most of what he was showing me, at least until he got to the attic with a big skylight he'd designed for a telescope. That's when Jason, who'd been building something complicated, looked up from his Legos and said, "a real telescope?"

Their conversation lasted almost an hour. Though it was less a conversation than a barrage of questions from Jason and patient answers from Chris.

"Jason," I said finally, "It's late ..."

"But Mom, it's Friday ..."

"Jason ..."

That's when Chris took the situation in hand and rolled up his blueprint. "I have to be going anyway, Jason," he said. "We'll talk more some other time, okay?"

What I remember is no word of protest from Jason. Just a look that you could almost describe as reverential.

On his way out, Chris hesitated. "Sorry if I came at a bad time." Then there was that intense look again. "I hope it works out. I'm looking forward to our being neighbors."

He came over again after he started construction carrying a rosebush. "It's a kind of peace offering," he said. "I'm going to be making a lot of noise for a while, shattering your peace and quiet, I'm afraid. I thought I'd apologize in advance."

"Thank you," I said, "But I think we're far enough away so the noise shouldn't be too much of a problem. I appreciate the thought, though, and I love roses."

"Good," he said. "I hope you'll come over and see how things are progressing. I'd like it if you did. I'd like us to get to know one another."

I looked into those clear eyes. Eyes that didn't seem capable of hiding anything. But then, I wasn't very good at judging those kinds of things, was I. Because I'd looked into other eyes once and thought the same thing.

"I don't think that's a good idea," I told him.

"Oh." He looked a little hurt and a little surprised. "Well ..." Then he looked at Jason, who had just come in from outside. "Maybe I can hire this guy to help me out once in a while." He grinned at Jason.

"You don't have to hire me," Jason said, smiling broadly back. "I want to help you out for free."

Remembering all this, I stop picking strawberries and stand there looking across the field at the walls of the new house. I think about the look on Jason's face, his happy enthusiasm. I think about my son's open heart, his open mind. I also think about his confusion when I wouldn't go over to see Chris's house with him, or when I told him it wasn't convenient to invite Chris over for dinner—even though I'd just picked up a large pizza and sodas, which we wouldn't finish ourselves, and it wasn't inconvenient at all.

I think about Chris, his grin, his intense look, the way his hands moved across the blueprint. I remember the hurt on his face when I told him we shouldn't get to know each other, and realize how he's respected that. How he's taught Jason how to play his guitar and find three constellations in the night sky.

Finally, I think about what Linda said about giving myself another chance. And how someone can go on hurting you only as long as you allow him to. Soon, I'm picking up the two full pails and carrying them to the kitchen, then I head across the field toward the sound of hammering and laughter.

"Hey, you two," I call out to them. Chris and Jason look up, surprised at first. Then Jason calls back, "Hey, Mom," and Chris says, "Hey, Katie."

"Could I interest you two in a little exchange?" I ask. "If you supply a grand tour, I'll supply a dinner for three, complete with strawberry pie."

Chris climbs down while Jason continues to hold the ladder. "I'm glad you decided to come over," Chris says.

I smile at him. "I am, too. It's just that for a while, it seemed a little further than it really is."

"Well, it doesn't matter as long as you're here now."

Jason jumps on top of a pile of plywood. "Can we have strawberry shortcake instead?" he asks. "I told Chris how awesome your biscuits are."

"Sure," I say, "with as much whipped cream as you want."

"Awesome," Chris and Jason say at the same time, and then we all burst out laughing and Chris holds his hand out to me. "Ready for your tour?" he asks.

"I think so." I look straight into his clear blue eyes, nod, take his strong hand. "Yes," I tell him. "I'm ready."

—

THE LOOK OF LOVE

Amy and Jill and I have dinner together every Thursday at *Mario's*. The three of us have been friends forever. Amy and I were bridesmaids at Jill's wedding two years ago, and Jill and I were Amy's attendants last year.

Tonight, it's my turn to be the center of attention.

"Okay, quiet, please," I tell them. "I have an announcement."

"I knew it!" Amy squeals. "Ted proposed last night, didn't he."

Jill puts her hand on my arm. "Did he, Cassie?"

"We're going to pick out a diamond on Saturday," I tell them.

"Pear," they both say at the same time, and we all laugh.

It's something we decided back in high school. Jill knew she wanted a round solitaire and Amy chose a marquise. Pear-shaped was the stone I set my heart on.

Saturday afternoon, Ted picks me up at one. He and I have known each other for ten years. Because our last names begin with 'H', we were in the same Home Room all through high school. We liked each other, but we never dated until we were both home from college our freshman year and ended up working at the same burger restaurant through Christmas break. I have no idea what happened during those months away from each other, but the second we saw each other again, fireworks went off. For him, for me. And three years later, they still are.

After we look at rings, we're going to head north to visit Ted's grandfather, and when we park near the jewelry store, Ted puts his hand on mine. "There's something I need to tell you," he says.

"When we get to Gramps' house, he intends to offer you Gram's ring."

"As my engagement ring?"

"That's what he said."

"But I can't take her ring. It's the only thing he has to remind him of her."

"I know," he says. "And when he called this morning to tell us, Mom tried to talk him out of it. But you know how stubborn Gramps is. So I've been thinking about it all morning and I know how happy it will make him if you take it. I mean, it won't be your engagement ring, but maybe you can put it on whenever we see him?"

"You mean take off my real engagement ring?" Somehow, it doesn't seem right. I want Ted to slip my ring on my finger and I never want to take it off. Ever. But I've known Gramps almost as long as I've known Ted. Gramps gave me a bouquet of violets from his garden when I graduated from college. I was there with Ted and Gramps when Grams died. And Ted and I have visited him every other Saturday ever since. "I'll accept the ring, if he insists," I tell Ted, but we can't lie to him. We can't let him think it's my engagement ring unless that's really what it's going to be."

Ted nods. "Okay. You're right. I'll explain that you have your heart set on a different ring. One that only belongs to you." He pats my hand. "He'll understand."

At the store, all the rings are beautiful and three of then are pear-shaped. But I can't decide which one I love best. "Take your time," the clerk says, "after all, it's something you'll wear always."

"You don't have to decide right now," Ted says. "We can come back tonight. Or tomorrow. Maybe it will be like us back then. A little time away and then when you see it again, you'll instantly know which one you want." Then we kiss each other lightly on the lips right there in front of the clerk.

Gramps is waiting on the porch when we come up the driveway. He comes down the steps and gives me the usual huge bear hug. Then he thumps Ted on the back. Inside, he has dinner ready … fried chicken, corn, and his own home-made biscuits. He tells us familiar stories—how he and Grams spent their honeymoon in a tent in Wyoming near Wind River Canyon. How Grams' chocolate cake was the best dessert in the universe, and how even though he knows she's not there, he still talks to her every day.

There are two photographs hanging over the mantel. One is of Gramps, young and handsome. The other is of Grams. She had huge brown eyes and lovely long hair piled on her head. The first time I saw it, my breath caught a little in my throat, because it could almost be me. Now that I'm used to it, I can see Ted in the curve of her mouth. There are other photographs on tables and bookcases. A whole lifetime of memories … the two of them growing older, children, grandchildren.

"You know," Gramps says, "the first time I ever saw you, I couldn't believe how much you look like her. And every time you come, it's almost like being with my Marion again."

Gramps and Ted both look at me, and I see the same thing in their eyes, a look of love … Gramps' for his Marion and Ted's for me.

Gramps reaches into his shirt pocket and takes out a ring. "Marion wore this all our life together." He holds it out to me. "I'd like you to have it."

"Gramps," Ted begins, "the thing is …"

"Oh, I know, I know. I understand that Cassie wants to pick out her own ring," Gramps says. Then he looks at me. "And you should. But it would make me very happy to know that this now belongs to you."

The ring is a princess-cut amethyst in a gold setting. It's not anything like the pear-shaped diamonds at the jeweler's. It's not the kind of ring that draws attention or sparkles on your finger.

"Do you remember how I couldn't make up my mind today?" I say to Ted. "Well, I just did."

I give the ring to Ted and hold out my left hand.

He looks at me hesitantly. "This is the ring you want?" he asks.

I nod, and he slips it on my finger.

It fits perfectly.

———

SOME LIKE IT HOT

Sometimes it seems like all my life Cathy's been begging me to do things I don't want to do. You'd think I'd be better now at saying no. But I start thinking about all the money I don't have in my checking account, and I begin to think maybe it's not such a bad idea after all.

"Look," Cathy says, "it's easy. Like playing dress-up. No one's going to know who you are under the makeup and wig. And it's a job. With a paycheck. So just say you'll do it, Julie, okay? You're perfect for it and you'll really be helping me out."

I say yes, because what else can I do? And the next afternoon I drive to her shop and when I open the door, a little bell jingles merrily. Everything's merry in Cathie's shop because it's all about good times and celebrations. If you want to have a party, Cathy's the person to call. She'll take care of everything— from napkins to food, from flowers to invitations. And she does such a good job, her business is growing faster than she can keep up with.

"Be right with you," Cathy calls from the back room.

"It's me," I tell her.

"Oh good," she says, "your costume's back here."

Phil comes in behind me. "Hi, Julie," he says, and gives me a peck on the cheek. "Cathy, I'm taking the five o'clock deliveries. They're all set, right?"

"Yes," she calls out, "all set."

He grabs bunches of balloons from a rack. "Wish I could hang around to see you do *this* one," he says, and winks. "I told Cathy to take a picture. Several pictures!" And then he's gone.

"What's the big deal about me in a costume?" I ask her. The sewing machine she's sitting at is going so fast, the colorful cloth flying through is almost a blur.

"Oh, you know Phil," she says. She points to a box on a table. "That's your costume. You'd better start getting ready, because it's halfway across town and you're supposed to be there at exactly six.

"Now hold on," I say, holding up the white halter dress. "This is no clown suit."

"Who said anything about a clown suit," she says. "These guys ordered Marilyn Monroe."

"Marilyn Monroe? Me? I can't be Marilyn Monroe!"

"Of course you can. She was a woman. You're a woman. She had great legs. You have great legs. She had a wonderful smile. You have a wonderful smile. And all the rest ... the voice, the hair ... was as phony as yours will be. Plus, how many times have we watched *Some Like It Hot*? Besides, you promised!!"

Half an hour later, I'm driving up Elm and thinking how much I really don't want to do this, and it doesn't help that people keep pulling up next to me and doing double-takes. Me, who eight weeks ago was wearing tailored gray suits and providing financial advice to Elton, Elton & Perry's conservative clientele. Now I'm Marilyn Monroe delivering balloons!

I pull into the apartment complex and park. All I want is to get this over with, go home, and never do anything like it again. I get out of the car, balloons in one hand, and peer at the numbers on the markers. Is it apartment 423 I'm looking for? Or 432? I start to unfold the work order, which promptly floats to the ground, and as I go to grab for it, the balloons float out of my hand toward the sky. I stand there and watch as a puff of wind blows them onto a fourth-floor deck. Now what??

I go inside and up the stairs to the fourth floor. I knock at the door and it swings open. "Hello?" I call out, and wait for an answer. Nothing. "Hello?" I call again. Still nothing. But I can hear water running, and someone singing, a man. A man singing in the shower. And I can see my balloons--across the living room through the glass sliders, caught on the deck. I stand there deliberating. Should I? Do I dare? I cross the living room, open the slider, grab the balloons, my heart pumping fiercely. And then the sound of the water stops.

I'm halfway back across the living room when someone comes through the open front door. A tall brunette. She sees me and gets a horrified look on her face. And then the bathroom door opens and out of a cloud of steam walks someone who looks like a Greek god, wearing nothing but a towel.

We all stare at each other for what feels like an eternity, and then the brunette ends it. "And I thought you'd changed!" she says to the Greek god. And then she turns and rushes back out through the door.

Now it's just the Greek god and me staring at one another, and I know I have to think of something fast. "Is it your birthday?" I ask.

He shakes his head.

"Whoops!" I say, "wrong apartment!"

I hear, "Hey … what … who …" just before I close the door behind me.

I find the right apartment. I'm only five minutes late. And since nothing could be any worse than what I've just been through, I do a pretty good job of being Marilyn. I hand the birthday boy the balloons, kiss his cheek, and leave a bright red lipstick mark, smile a lot, and pose for pictures with the guests. In thirty minutes it's time for me to back out the door blowing kisses. When I get home, there's a message from Latham & Burke offering me a second interview at nine o'clock the next morning.

I arrive for the interview ten minutes early and am invited into a conference room with a round table around which several people are sitting. I'm introduced to them all, and I remember to be confident, competent, businesslike, and engaging. At least until I get to the final introduction. Then my confident smile slips and I stammer. Greek god extends his hand, and I hear him saying *you and your balloons!* But actually, all he says is, *Nice to meet you.*

I nod. His name is Brad or Brian or Bruce. The interview goes on forever and I never make eye contact with him, although I can feel him looking at me, *really* looking. But when I do glance his way once, he's doodling on a notebook, and the page he's doodling on is covered with balloons.

I get the job. I have my own small but comfortable office. Best of all, I won't ever have to be Marilyn Monroe again. And then, after I've been there for a week, there's a knock on my door. "Yes?" I say. "Hi," he says, poking his head in. "I'm Brian. We met at your interview."

"Yes, I remember. Nice to see you again."

"Have you got some time to go over some files?"

"Sure." I sit there.

"In my office," he says.

"Whoops." I jump up "Of course."

He looks at me. "Funny," he says, "for a second there..." He frowns. "Have we ever met ? I mean, before your interview?"

I shake my head. "No, I don't think so."

"I don't know. You remind me of someone ..."

"I've been told I have that kind of face," I say.

"No. It's not that kind of face. It's a very nice face. I just mean ..." He shrugs. "I don't know what I mean." Then he laughs a little. "Now you're going to think I'm some kind of idiot. So if you don't mind, can we start over? Hi, I'm Brian. We met at your interview. I was wondering if we could go over some client lists in my office?"

All afternoon I keep waiting for him to come through the door again and point his finger at me. "I remember who you are!" But he doesn't. And since every time my mind wanders I see him stepping out of all that steam and see that brunette storming out of his apartment, I realize that there are some men you just have to learn to stay away from.

He makes that hard, though. Because first thing the next morning, he asks me out to lunch.

"Sorry," I say, "but I'm working at my desk through lunch. So much to catch up on, so much to do!" I fling my arm across my desk to bring his attention to all the files sitting there and knock my coffee right into the wastebasket. "Whoops!" I say.

He stares at me. "Tomorrow?"

"I'm planning to work through lunch every day this week."

"How about Saturday? They're doing a retrospective of 50s movies downtown. Saturday they're playing *Some Like It Hot*."

"*Some Like It Hot?*"

"Yeah," he says, "you know. Marilyn Monroe?"

"Right."

"Well ... maybe some other time?" and then he's gone.

He knows. And even if he doesn't, I have to get it out in the open. I practically broke into his apartment and I probably ruined his relationship with the brunette. So I owe him an explanation. But also, she told me something about him that I can't forget. She saw *me* and said he hadn't changed one bit. Which means he's one of those Greek gods who has lots of women, and at least occasionally, has them at the same time. So I also owe him the truth that I'll never go out with him. Ever.

The next afternoon after an entire morning with a client, I see Brian coming toward me down the hallway. I start walking faster, thinking I can get to my office door before we meet. And I'm right. Except when I open the door, I can't get inside. Because my office is filled with balloons. A zillion helium balloons.

I feel him behind me, turn around. He's smiling.

"Well, I say, "when did you figure it out?"

"When I couldn't get either one of you off my mind," he says. "You or Marilyn. But mostly it was your habit of saying 'whoops.' Plus, just to be sure, I asked someone at Cathy's Parties who the pretty girl is who plays Marilyn. He told me it was Julie, but she was no longer available to do Marilyn anymore because she just got another job."

"It was an honest mistake," I say. "The balloons got away from me and got caught on your deck and your door was open and then your girlfriend came in and then she left before I could say anything." I shrug. "Big whoops. Did you straighten it out with her? Do you need me to talk to her?"

"Not necessary," he says. "There's nothing to straighten out. Melanie and I hadn't seen each other in a couple of years. She just happened to be in town and, apparently, hasn't changed a bit."

"*She* hasn't changed?"

"Jealous," he says. "Of my secretary, my sister, my best friend, Rob, my cat, anyone and everyone. Even, I guess, of Marilyn Monroe."

We smile at each other.

"So now that we're on a footing that's fair and square," he says, "would you reconsider? Come out with me to the movies this weekend?"

I reach behind me and grab a balloon. I hand it to him. It happens to be a silver Mylar with a zillion red hearts all over it.

———

THE PERFECT WOMAN

Okay, so maybe what I did that day was a little out of line. But everyone has his breaking point, right? I mean, it had only been forty-eight hours since my girlfriend Maryanne dumped me for the guy who sold her his mountain bike.

On top of all that, my boss had called me into his office to tell me my promotion would be held up. Again.

So I wasn't in a good mood when I walked into my apartment after work. And the fact that it was filled with smoke was the straw that broke the camel's back.

Then my brother Alan dropped by for a visit.

"Look, Greg," he said, "why don't you just close the sliding door and ignore it? The guy's just cooking dinner."

"Easy for you" I said. "You don't happen to live in the same building with him."

I thought about the last time I went down there and banged on Julian's door, asked him not to put his barbecue under my sliding glass door, told him the smoke comes pouring in like the whole place is on fire.

I looked up at the smoke rolling along the ceiling and something sort of snapped. I went into the kitchen and got a gallon pitcher full of water. Alan watched me. He didn't have a clue until I slid back the screen door and stepped out onto the balcony. But by then, it was too late.

It was a direct hit.

After about four minutes, there was a knock on the door. I opened it. We stared at each other. She was holding a wet steak on a fork, and she didn't look happy.

"Was that some kind of bizarre accident?" she said. "Or did you just put out my grill on purpose?"

It took a second for my mind to start working again. "Not your grill," I said, "Julian's grill. I've asked him twice now not to smoke me out, and he keeps on doing it."

"I have no idea what you're talking about," she said. "All I know is that this was my first dinner in my new apartment." She held the steak a little higher.

A lot of things started going through my head right about then. That I'd really put my foot in it this time. That life was out to get me. That she had incredibly creamy skin, shiny dark hair, and huge gray eyes. That what I'd done wasn't the best way to make a good impression.

So I did what any decent guy would do when a good-looking woman thinks he's the biggest jerk she's seen in a decade. I stammered. And that's when Alan stepped in and did what he does best. Saved the day. For himself.

"Greg here is a little hard to control sometimes," Alan said. "But he didn't know it was your steak down there. This guy Julian, the one who was living downstairs before you, was pretty hard to take." Then he gave her his very best *you and I understand how things are* smile. He stepped past me into the hall, looked at the steak and shook his head. "I'd like to make this up somehow," he said. "Since you just moved in, you probably haven't tried that steak-house up on the corner...?"

Next thing I knew, they were gone. Together.

He called later that night. To tell me that Kris was amazing—not just great-looking but smart, funny, interesting—the perfect woman.

"Greg," he said, "no hard feelings, right? I mean, I haven't had a date in ten days. And you've got Maryanne."

I thought about Maryanne riding her new mountain bike in tandem with somebody else. "So her name is Kris," I said. "Right."

The next day was Saturday, and I decided to get away from it all. I dragged my kayak out of the basement and tied it on top of my jeep. I was tying the last knot when Kris pulled into the parking space next to mine. She got out of her car and I turned to face her. "I'm sorry about what happened," I told her. "The water. The steak. The fact that Alan got to take you out."

I thought I saw the beginnings of a smile. I held out my hand. "No hard feelings?"

"No hard feelings," she said. She reached up and patted the kayak. "So you like kayaking. It's something I always thought I'd like to ..."

But she didn't get a chance to finish because Alan pulled up. "Give me two minutes," she said to him. Then she looked at me. "Have fun!" And then she ran inside.

"So," I said to Alan, "another date already, huh?"

He nodded. "Antiquing."

***

When I got back on Sunday, I felt better. There's something about sleeping in a tent and giving yourself over to a fast-moving river that helps put things in perspective. But there was still something I wanted to do. I went to the grocery store, bought a steak, then went back and knocked on her door.

"Reparations," I said, offering her the steak when she answered.

She hefted it. "That's a pretty big one," she said. "About twice as big as the one you ruined. How about if I cook it and we share it?"

I looked at her creamy skin, her gorgeous gray eyes. It hurt like hell to turn her down. "Previous engagement," I said. "I'm really sorry." And I was really really sorry.

79

After that, we ran into each other often. In the laundry room, the parking lot, the gym. She was always friendly, and I began to think that fate was sticking it to me. First, I'd lost Maryanne for no reason I could figure out. And now there was this friendly, beautiful, dynamite girl, who was seeing my brother and constantly there every time I turned around. She even started running the same route I ran every morning. Sometimes I'd see her up ahead, running slow enough so I knew I was going to catch up with her. But then I'd turn around and go back the way I'd come, even though it doubled the run and made me late for work. Every time I saw her, I felt guilty. Like I was trying to beat Alan's time. And probably that's exactly what I wanted to do. But I couldn't make myself do it.

One Friday night, she did it again. The grill. The smoke. I couldn't believe it. I got up and closed the sliding glass door and tried not to think about it.

After fifteen minutes or so, there was a knock at the door. "Haven't you noticed anything?" Kris said.

She walked across the living room, over to the door, slid it open. A cloud of smoke almost made her disappear.

"Look," I said, "exactly what is this all about?"

"I was trying to get your attention," she said. "Why do I get the feeling you're avoiding me? You're the one who made the lousy first impression. Aren't you anxious to fix it? I mean, I had a right to be mad that first day, didn't I? But haven't you noticed I've been trying to be friendly ever since?"

I looked at her. "The thing is," I said, "I have a couple of scruples left, and one of them is that I don't horn in on another guy's relationship, especially when the other guy's my brother."

She didn't say anything for a second, but her eyes got very dark. "You really think I'd do something like that?"

"Something like what?"

"Throw myself at my boyfriend's brother??" Then she hustled out and slammed the door behind her.

I decided to avoid her as much as I could after that. But I only saw her once in two weeks, and that was just catching a glimpse as she drove out of the parking area. She was never in the laundry. Never in the gym. Twice I saw her running in the evening.

Then Alan called one night. "I ran into Maryanne today," he said. "How come you didn't tell me?"

"I didn't really want to talk about it," I said.

"Yeah," he said, "I know what you mean. Anyway, I figured you'd find out from Kris soon enough."

"Find out what?"

"She didn't tell you she decided I was a jerk?"

"Smart girl," I said.

***

I begin running in the evening. Working out in the morning. Doing my laundry on Sunday instead of Monday, even though there was always a long wait for a machine. But every time I bumped into her, she ignored me. Then one day I found her in the pool, practicing rolls in her new kayak. Her form was lousy and she kept coming up halfway instead of doing a complete roll. After six tries, she didn't come up at all on the seventh.

I dove in and righted the kayak, but she wasn't in it. Then she popped up on the other side, coughing.

"You okay?" I asked.

"Oh sure," she said, "just half-drowned."

I dove under the kayak and came up beside her. "C'mon," I said. "I'll show you how to do it the right way."

There was no one in the pool, no one around at all. The water lapped against the kayak. Her ear was near my mouth. "I figured you and Alan were seeing each other," I said, "and I was trying to stay out of the way. Avoid temptation. And I was so stuck on that, I missed all the right signals. I know you're not the kind of person who hits on her boyfriend's brother. But do you have an idea how hard it was for me not to hit on my brother's girl? At least when the girl was you?"

She smiled.

"Can we start over?" I asked.

"You mean the bar-b-que, the steak, the water?"

"Nah. I figured we could skip all that since we've already had our first fight. Move into some of the better things a relationship has to offer."

I put my arms around her, looked into those beautiful gray eyes and decided, what the heck. If anyone came to use the pool, they'd get the idea pretty quick and just decide to come back later.

—

BOOKS BY THIS AUTHOR

SHORT STORY COLLECTIONS

AFTERNOON DELIGHT BOOK ONE

AFTERNOON DELIGHT BOOK TWO

AFTERNOON DELIGHT BOOK THREE

AFTERNOON DELIGHT BOOK FOUR

AFTERNOON DELIGHT BOOK FIVE

COW HORMONES

NOVELS

CLICK

DON'T LOOK DOWN

A DANCE WITH THE DEVIL

PAYBACK

LOVE CANAL

RIDDLE

STINKBUG

50 ACRES MORE OR LESS

MOON OF THE DARK RED CALVES

www.ingramcontent.com/pod-product-compliance
Lightning Source LLC
Chambersburg PA
CBHW020637130626
46552CB00003B/1273